She Never Stopped Talking

By

SUSAN L. PARE'

This book is a work of fiction. Names, characters, places, and incidents are either the product of the author's imagination or are used fictionally. Any resemblance to an actual person, living or dead, or the actual events or locales is entirely coincidental.

Printed in the United States of America.

First Edition: August 2019

Cover designed by Susan L. Pare'

ISBN-13: 978-1-7335572-2-1

MORE BOOKS BY THIS AUTHOR

Red

The House on Ludington Street

What's Behind the Screen Door?

The Mayor's Son

Willerton Woods

Cowtown

Floating Face Down
A Sheriff "Cowboy" Berkson Mystery Novel – Book Three

Let's Play Autopsy

A Bad Week In Hollister
A Sheriff "Cowboy" Berkson Mystery Novel – Book Two

Don't Smother Your Mother
A Sheriff "Cowboy" Berkson Mystery Novel – Book One

Crossing Sydney

Table of Contents

Dedication

Thank you, Steve Tichenor

It's strange how friends are made. It's stranger still that you can consider someone you've never met a friend. Like Steve. I've never met Steve in person. He resides in the beautiful state of Oregon and we are many miles apart. We connected through the media a few years back and I've thoroughly enjoyed getting to know him.

Steve has a great sense of humor, which is probably what drew me to him. It can be dry and pretty weird at times, like mine. On many occasions, I start my day laughing due to some absolutely ridiculous joke that he sent me. And, then, he'll send me some heartbreaking story to read, which will make my eyes leak.

He's intelligent, well-read, respectful, funny, compassionate, and truly loves our country. I am so glad I have him in my life.

Steve helped me in my journey of getting this novel published and I am grateful for his assistance. I'm honored to dedicate this book to Steve and wish to thank him for his kindness.

Thank you, Steve. You're one in a million.

She Never Stopped Talking

May

Prom Night

"What the hell?" Blake Armstrong exclaimed, as he rolled over and glanced at the clock on the nightstand. "It's one-thirty in the morning," he muttered. "Who the hell could that be?"

"Maybe Kari forgot her key," Nichole mumbled as she reached up and turned on a light. "Do you want me to get it?"

"No," Blake answered. "Stay here. I'll see who it is."

Nichole watched as her husband grabbed his robe and walked out of the room to answer the door. A few moments later, Nichole heard loud voices coming from the living room. Concerned, she jumped out of bed, threw on her robe, and ran to see what was happening.

As she entered the living room, she saw two police officers helping Blake to the couch

"No!" Blake sobbed. "It has to be a mistake."

"What's a mistake?" Nichole asked.

"I'm sorry, but there's been an accident, ma'am," one of the officers told her.

"Oh, my God. Please, tell me nothing has happened to one of the kids."

"It's Kari," Blake told her. "She's been in an accident and it's bad. They don't think she's going to make it, Nichole."

Nichole grabbed the back of a chair and braced herself. "What kind of an accident?" she asked the policemen.

"It was a car accident. I'm sorry, ma'am but the driver didn't make it and . . ."

"Was it Logan Sands? Kari went to the prom with him tonight."

"Yes, ma'am. I'm sorry to say he was killed instantly."

"Oh, dear God, no. What about his parents? Do his parents know yet?"

"I believe they are being notified right now."

Nichole took a deep breath and let it out. "I need to go to her," she said, trying to calm down. "Please, tell me, where have they taken my daughter?"

One

December – Seven Months Later

Nichole looked over at her daughter and sighed. "Come on, Kari," she said softly. "Wake up, will you? Enough already. We need you to come back to us."

"She can hear you, you know. One of these days she just might answer you."

Nichole jumped at the sound of the man's voice. She turned and smiled. "You scared me."

"Sorry."

Nichole glanced over at Kari and shook her head. "How can you be so sure she hears me?"

"I've had patients that have been in comas for hours and some for years. Almost all of them have said that they remember people talking to them. I'm pretty sure that Kari knows you're talking to her."

"I don't know, Doctor. I'd like to think so, but sometimes I think I'm wishing my life away. It's been over six months since the accident. Maybe, I should give in to Blake's wishes and let her go."

Dr. Ben Campbell pulled a chair over next to Nichole and sat down. "When I was a teenager, I had a friend who was in a car accident and sustained injuries much like what Kari has experienced. It happened on a Christmas Eve. Seven years she was in a coma, Nichole. She hung on for seven years. Finally, her parents gave up and made the decision to pull the plug - so to speak - and you know what happened?"

Nichole shook her head no.

"She woke up. Just like that. No warning. Nothing."

Nichole glanced up at him. “And?”

“When she went home, she found her Christmas presents waiting for her. All wrapped up just like they had been seven years ago. Her parents had so much faith that she’d wake up and come home that they never threw the gifts out or changed a thing in her room. Everything was exactly the same.” Dr. Campbell smiled. “So, to answer your question. Well, Nichole, I had dinner with her and her husband last week. So, don’t you give up yet, you hear?”

Nichole smiled. “I won’t. It’s just that it gets hard sometimes, you know.”

Dr. Campbell stood and put his hand on Nichole’s shoulder. “I know. But, hang in there a little longer. You never know what God has planned for you. And, for Kari.”

“Thanks, Ben. I need a little pep talk now and then.”

“How’s your boy doing?”

“Keith is fine. He misses his sister, of course, but he’s doing okay.”

“Good. And, how is Blake? I don’t see him here very often.”

“He comes when he can. Mostly after work. He’s working long hours, trying to stay on top of everything. I don’t know how much longer the insurance is going to pay for Kari’s medical bills.”

“If you reach that point, let me know. We’ll work something out. Well, I’ve got to finish my rounds. I’ll talk to you later.”

“Bye.” Nichole watched him walk out of the room and down the hall. She wanted to cry, but as she felt the tears gathering in the corners of her eyes she straightened up in her chair and took a deep breath. "Not today," she whispered to the quiet room. "Today is not the day for tears."

Nichole stood and pushed her chair closer to her daughter's hospital bed. She reached over and took Kari's hand and squeezed it. "I can't believe how long your hair has grown," she told her daughter. "Do you know you have a streak of gray hair on the left side of your head? What I think is puzzling is that your head injury was on the right side. Funny, isn't it? You'd think the hair on the right side would come in gray, but, oh, no. Not with you. You always have to do things differently from everyone else. But, it's kind of pretty, you know?"

Nichole ran her hand through Kari's hair, smoothing it back from her face. "Actually, the streak is more white than gray. I like it."

Suddenly, Nichole felt a slight chill run through her body. She stood up, walked over to the windows, and looked outside. "It's nice out today. The sun is shining and it's warm out. In fact, it's almost warm enough to go without a jacket."

Nichole felt another chill, making her shiver. She turned and looked back at Kari. "Is that you doing that, Kari? Are you trying to get through to me?"

Seven months, Nichole thought. I've been here every day for the past seven months and I may be here in this room for another seven months. Or, years even. How long do I wait? Are there any rules to go by? God, I hate this. Not knowing what's going to happen day after day. Should I listen to Blake and let her go? Would that be the humane thing to do?

She glanced over at the mirror on the wall and shook her head in disgust. I'm old, she thought. I've aged ten years in the past seven months.

"Stop it!" she said to herself. "Feeling sorry for yourself doesn't help any."

She walked back to her daughter's bed and reached for a book that was on the nightstand. "How about I read you a little more of My Cousin Rachel?" she asked Kari. "You know we're almost finished with it. Would you like that?" She opened the novel and started to read to her daughter.

An hour later, tears streaming down her cheeks, Nichole closed the book. "I swore I wasn't going to cry today and here I am, crying like a baby. I can't remember the last time I cried over a book."

Nichole glanced down at Kari and smiled. "Did you enjoy that? What do you . . ." She stared at Kari, not believing what she was seeing. Rolling down the side of Kari's face was a single tear. Kari was crying.

Nichole jumped out of the chair and ran down the hallway to the nurses' station. "Come see," she yelled at the nurse sitting behind the counter.

"What is it, Mrs. Armstrong? What do you want me to see?"

"It's Kari. I think she's awake. I was reading to her and she started crying. Come see."

Betty walked around the counter and followed Nichole to Kari's room. She walked over to the bed and checked Kari's vitals. She turned and looked at Nichole and shook her head. "I'm sorry, Mrs. Armstrong, but I don't think there have been any changes."

Nichole stared at her, obviously upset. "But she was crying. I saw her cry. Why would she cry if she wasn't awake?"

"I have no idea. However, she's not crying now. I'll make a note for the doctor. Perhaps he can tell you."

"But . . ." Nichole turned away from the nurse, trying to compose herself. She took a deep breath and let it out. She turned back and smiled at Betty. "Wishful thinking, I guess. I'm sorry I bothered you."

Betty put her arm around Nichole and gave her a hug. "I just wish it were true."

"I'm going to go get some coffee. Can I bring you anything?"

"No thanks, I'm fine," Betty replied. "Take your time. I'll keep an eye on Kari."

Nichole sat down at a table in the hospital cafeteria. It was the middle of the afternoon and there were only a couple of people in the room getting a mid-day snack. She took a sip of her coffee and closed her eyes, breathing deeply. I'm beginning to wonder if I really did see a tear on Kari's cheek, she thought. I'm so tired, perhaps I'm seeing things.

Her mind wandered back to the night of Kari's accident. She could still picture Kari standing in front of the fireplace, with Logan at her side, while their pictures were taken. Kari looked so beautiful in her long yellow dress. Logan had given her a wrist corsage with small yellow roses, and she had given him a boutonniere with matching flowers.

Kari had been so happy that night, Nichole recalled. It was her senior prom and, in a few weeks, she would be graduating high school. It was an exciting time for her and she couldn't wait to move on to college and a new exciting life.

Then, in an instant, it all changed.

At first, the police thought it had been a hit-and-run. Most likely, they said, it was a drunk driver who was afraid to stop and help for fear of being arrested. But the accident didn't happen like the police originally thought. They discovered that Logan's car had been hit in the back, pushing it off the road and headfirst into a tree. Logan was killed instantly and Kari . . . Well, she might as well be dead, Nichole thought and immediately pushed the horrible thought from her mind, shaking her head in disgust.

Logan and Kari were in that car for almost an hour before they were found. If only those witnesses had stopped to help . . . Or, even come forward sooner. But, no. Too afraid to get involved. The rotten bastards should be rotting in jail, but they didn't even get a slap on the wrist.

Nichole reached for her cup, took another sip of her coffee, and made a face. It was cold. She looked around the cafeteria and realized that, except for her, it was empty. How long have I been sitting here, she wondered, as she glanced at her watch.

Two

"Will you stop it?" Keith yelled. "Just once I'd like to eat a meal without you two fighting about Kari."

Nichole looked over at her son, shocked at his outburst. Her quiet, laid-back son never raised his voice and she realized that he had reached his breaking point. "I'm sorry, Keith," she said softly.

"It's constant, you know. Every night it's the same fight. Pull the plug, don't pull the plug. I'm sick of it."

Blake looked at Keith, his face red from being so angry at his wife. "I don't care for your tone of voice, Keith. This has nothing to do with you."

"Seriously, Dad? I'm still part of this family, you know. I have to listen to this shit day after day."

"Watch your language, Keith," Nichole told him.

Keith shook his head in disgust and stood up. "I'm out of here."

"You're not going anywhere," his father said. "Sit down and finish your dinner."

Keith stared at him.

"Now!" Blake yelled at him.

Keith straightened up his six-foot-two-inch body and shook his head no. "I don't think so," he stated and walked away from the table.

"Keith! Get back here," Blake yelled and, then, heard the front door slam shut.

Nichole threw her napkin on her plate and sat back. "Are you happy now? You just drove the only child we have left out the door?"

"Our only child? Did Kari die today and you forgot to tell me?"

"You know what I meant. He's right, you know?"

"Who's right?"

"Keith, of course. All we do is fight, Blake. It's the same fight over and over. I don't know if I can take it much longer."

"Then, make a fucking decision. You need to let her go. We're going broke. While I'm working my ass off to try to pay the bills, you're spending all your time at the hospital talking to a dead person. She's gone, Nichole, and it's time you accepted that fact."

"For God's sake, Blake, how can you say that? Kari isn't dead. Dr. Campbell says there's a good chance that she will wake up one of these days."

"Of course, he does. The longer she's in that coma the more money is in his pocket."

Nichole glared at him, holding back the tears. "That is a horrible thing to say."

"We don't have a marriage anymore. All we do is fight. We're going to lose Keith, too, if this crap keeps up."

Nichole looked away, trying to keep the tears at bay. "You're right, Blake. It's got to stop." Nichole stood up and started to clear the table.

"Can I help?" Blake asked.

"I've got it. I'm going back to the hospital after I do the dishes. Do you want to come with me and spend some time with your daughter?"

"Why don't you stay home tonight and get some rest? You were with Kari all day. It won't hurt for you to stay home one night and spend some time here with me. Besides, she doesn't know if we are here or there."

Nichole smiled. "I'm sorry I neglect you. Really, Blake, I mean it. It's just that – never mind." She hesitated a moment. "Well, do you?"

"Do I what?" Blake replied.

"Do you want to come with me to see your daughter or not?"

"Not tonight, Nichole. Why don't you just leave? I'll do the dishes." Blake responded.

"Are you sure?" Nichole asked.

Blake looked up at her and shook his head, his disappointment in her decision obvious. "Oh, I'm sure. Just go."

Nichole sat next to Kari, holding her hand. The room was dark except for a small light over Kari's bed. She looked at her daughter and smiled. She's so beautiful, Nichole thought. Except for her hair, she doesn't look a day older than she did seven months ago. Nichole closed her eyes and started to drift off when suddenly the room filled with light.

"Sorry, Mrs. Armstrong, but it's time for Kari's meds and she needs to be turned on her other side," Jeanne, the night nurse, told Nichole.

Nichole stood up and walked to the end of the bed, watching the nurse as she injected medications into Kari's feeding tube. "Does she have physical therapy in the morning?" Nichole asked the nurse.

"I believe she is scheduled for it. I can check if you want," Jeanne replied.

"Please. I've got some errands to run in the morning and I'd like to do them while Kari is getting her p.t."

"I'll check for you when I'm done here. By the way, we just put on a fresh pot of coffee, if you'd like to go get a cup."

Nichole hesitated a moment. "That sounds good. I think I will get a cup," she finally said, turned, and walked out of the room.

An hour later Nichole stood up and stretched. Time to go home and try to get some sleep, she thought. Kari was resting comfortably and there was nothing more Nichole could do at the hospital. She dreaded the thought of facing Blake, knowing that another fight was sure to ensue.

She glanced over at the small couch in Kari's room. Without giving it a second thought, she slipped off her shoes, laid down, and curled up into a ball. Within seconds she was asleep.

At midnight, a man walked into the room and looked down at Nichole, who was sleeping soundly on the couch. He took a small blanket from the end of Kari's bed and gently covered Nichole with it. "Sleep well, Nichole," he whispered and walked out of the room.

Three

Nichole was awakened by Jeanne checking on Kari. She sat up on the couch and yawned. "I guess I fell asleep," she said. "What time is it?"

"It's just a little after four," the nurse told her. "I thought I'd check in on Kari one more time before I leave."

Nichole was surprised by the time. "I can't believe it. The last I remember it was around nine or so. I actually slept for almost seven hours. I think that's the most sleep I've had at one time in over six months."

"I guess you must have needed it," the nurse said. She made a notation on the chart and headed for the door. "Do you need anything? We've got coffee if you want some."

"No thanks. I've got to go home and check in with Blake. He must be worried about me."

"He knows you're here. He called around ten and asked if you were still here. He had been trying to call you and was concerned that you weren't answering your phone. When I told him you were sleeping, he said not to wake you."

"Thanks, Jeannie."

"No problem. See you tomorrow?"

"I'll be here."

"Why don't you just rent a room at the hospital? Then, you'd never have to come home."

Nichole jumped at the sound of Blake's voice. She shut the front door and walked into the living room.

Blake was sitting in a lounge chair with a cup of coffee in his hand. "You scared me," Nichole told him.

"You could have called and told me you weren't coming home," Blake said angrily. "I was worried about you."

"I didn't plan on staying there all night. I fell asleep. I'm sorry."

"Keith didn't come home last night."

Nichole looked surprised. "What do you mean, he didn't come home? Where is he?"

"I don't know."

"Well, did you call his friends? What about Casey? Did you call her?"

Blake stood up and laughed.

"What's funny?" Nichole asked.

"Look at you. You haven't paid any attention to Keith in months. Now, all of sudden, you're concerned about someone besides Kari."

Suddenly, Nichole sat down on the couch and started to sob. The tears that she had been holding back for months flowed like water from a broken dam.

Blake stared at her for a moment, then walked over to her and put his arms around her. "I'm sorry. That wasn't fair of me."

Nichole continued to sob, her body shaking with the grief that had consumed her for so long. Finally, she pulled back from Blake's arms and whispered, "Ti . . . Tis . . ."

"What?"

"Tissue. I need a tissue."

"I'll get you one."

Half an hour later, Nichole and Blake were sitting across the kitchen table from each other. Blake smiled at her. "Do you feel any better?"

Nichole smiled back at him. "I do."

"I was beginning to think that you were made of steel. I mean, like, really hard steel. You needed to get that out of your system, Nichole. You're not alone in this, you know. Keith and I are hurting just as much as you are. We're all in this together and we should be here for each other. You can lean on me, you know. Let me be your rock for a while. It's okay to cry. We are letting this drive us apart and I don't want to lose you or this family."

"Me either. It's just that I thought I had to be strong for you and Keith. And, I'm . . ."

Blake looked at her. "You're what?"

"I'm just so tired all the time."

"We all are," Blake said, smiling. "I have an idea if you're up to listening to it."

"What's that?" Nichole said yawning.

"Actually, I'd like Keith to be here when I tell you. Let's wait until he gets home. Are you okay with that?"

Nichole yawned again, then, smiled. "Good idea. I'm so tired I probably wouldn't remember what you said anyway."

"Why don't you go lie down for a while? See if you can get a few hours of sleep."

Nichole reached across the table and took her husband's hand. "I think I will. And, Blake, I'm so sorry for the way I've been acting."

"Me, too, Babe. I guess we've both been a couple of jackasses."

Nichole grinned. “Well, I don’t know if I’d go that far.”

“Well, idiots, then. Is that better?”

“Whatever. And, I think I will go lie down for a while if you don’t mind.”

“Wait a minute,” Blake said as Nichole started to walk out of the kitchen. “I almost forget to tell you something.”

“Can’t it wait?” she inquired.

“No. It’s important. Sheriff Katts called.”

Nichole turned and stared at him. “What did he want?” she asked, as her heart started beating faster.

“They found the other car. The one that caused the accident.”

“Are you fucking kidding me?” she yelled.

“What?”

“You almost forgot to tell me?” she shouted. “What the hell, Blake?”

“I’m sorry. And, calm down, will you? I guess I was so concerned about you that it slipped my mind for a moment.”

“I’m sorry I yelled,” she said, lowering her voice. “Where did they find the car?”

“It’s been hidden in a garage since the accident,” Blake told her.

“Whose garage?” she murmured.

“You remember Hunter Douglas, don’t you?” Blake asked her.

“Of course, I remember him. Kari dated him a while back.” Suddenly the realization of what Blake was saying hit her. “Oh, my God! Are you saying it was Hunter that ran them off the road?”

"The police think so. The car is his father's and it hasn't been driven since that night. I'm guessing that Hunter was driving it the night of the accident."

"How did the police find it?" Nichole asked.

"The paint. This is why it's taken so long to find the car. They got a paint match off of Logan's car and tracked down every car in town that had that kind of paint. Katts figures that Hunter's dad hid the car in the garage to protect his kid."

"Why, Blake? Why would Hunter do it?"

"Your guess is as good as mine. Although, I do remember that he wasn't too happy when Kari broke up with him. Revenge, maybe? Who knows? They haven't arrested Hunter yet, though. They need more proof that he was the one driving it. They're checking to see if he used the car to go to the prom that night. Anyway, it looks like it won't be long before they know for sure."

"Who else would have been driving it if not Hunter?" Nichole questioned.

"There are other kids in that family who drive. Anyway, we'll find out soon enough. Now, go get some rest," Blake said.

"Right. Like I could sleep now."

Four

"We don't know where your brother is," Nichole told Kari. "He was really upset when he stormed out of the house on Tuesday. I can't blame him for being angry but he should have gotten over it by now. He's been gone two nights now. You'd think he'd at least call us and let us know if he's okay."

Nichole picked up a book off Kari's nightstand and glanced at it, wondering where it came from. She noticed a note stuck between the pages of the book, removed it, and read it out loud. "Nichole, I noticed that you enjoy reading Daphne du Maurier novels to Kari. I thought she might enjoy this one. Ben."

She glanced over at Kari, smiling. "Well, wasn't that nice of him? I think we lucked out when we got him for your doctor, Kari. How many doctors do you know who would take the time to go out and buy a patient a gift, much less even notice what they enjoy?"

She opened the book and flipped through the pages. "It's Rebecca. I don't recall reading this one before. I'll start it later if you don't mind. I have to leave for a little while. I promised your dad that I'd pick up a few groceries for tonight and I've got a hair appointment at ten. I'll be back after that."

Nichole bent down and kissed her daughter on her forehead. "I love you," she told her, smiling sadly.

On the way out of the hospital, Nichole called Blake on her cell phone. The call went straight to voice mail. "Hi, honey," she said into her phone. "Just wondering if you've heard from Keith? I'm getting more worried every hour that we don't hear from him. Also, I'm planning on dinner around six-thirty. Love you."

Nichole had no more ended her call before her phone rang. "Blake? That was fast. I just called you."

"I know. I couldn't get to my phone in time."

"Did you listen to my voice message?" Nichole asked him.

"No. Did you hear from Keith?"

"Not a word. I was hoping that you had," she answered.

"This is getting serious, Nichole. I know he's seventeen and perfectly capable of taking care of himself but for him to be gone this long and not check in with us isn't like him."

"I agree. Listen, Blake, I've got a few errands to run. They shouldn't take long and, as soon as I'm done with those, I'm going to start calling his friends. Someone has to know where he is."

"You'd think so, wouldn't you," Blake responded. "Well, call me if you find out anything. I think if we don't hear from him by dinner time, we should call the police."

Nichole hesitated, thinking about what Blake had said. "Seriously, Blake? You really think he could be in trouble?"

"God only knows. It's almost forty-eight hours since he left and we haven't heard from him. I think this is serious, Nichole."

"Let me make those phone calls before you do anything. Maybe he's just punishing us for the way we've been acting. Being with Kari has been a priority since her accident and we have been ignoring him."

"To be honest, Nichole, we've both been shitty parents to him these past few months. Let's just hope he comes home soon or that we at least find out where he's staying."

"I'll check with all his friends and let you know if I find out anything."

"Good. I've got to go. Love you," Blake told her.

"Love you, too," Nichole said, ending the call.

"That's it. I don't know who else to call," Nichole told Kari. "I've called every one of his friends that I could think of. I even talked to Pastor Jenkins, Keith's swim coach, and his old girlfriends, which was a waste of time. No one has seen or heard from him since Tuesday. I'm at my wit's end, Kari."

Nichole sat on the small couch, staring at her phone. "I guess I better call your dad," she said. "He said if we don't hear from Keith by dinner time, we would have to get the police involved." She took a deep breath and let it out. "This really sucks," she mumbled and called Blake.

"I can't eat," Blake said as he pushed his plate away. "I'm calling Sheriff Katts right now."

Nichole sat back in her chair and looked over at him. "I know. It's just that if we call him, we're accepting the fact that something may have happened to Keith. I don't think I could handle it if he's . . ." Nichole put her face in her hands and started to cry.

"We have checked with everyone we can think of. We can't do this by ourselves, Nichole. We need help and the longer we go, without doing anything to find him, the more serious it could become."

Nichole shook her head in agreement. "I know. Go ahead and call Carson." Suddenly, her body shuddered.

"Are you okay?" Blake asked.

She gave him a puzzling look. "No. I don't know. I felt like someone was walking over my grave. It gave me the shivers."

Blake picked up his cell phone and made the call. "It's ringing," he told Nichole.

She watched him, noting that she hadn't seen him look this upset since the night Kari was in the accident.

"Yes, hello. Is Sheriff Katts there?" He waited for a reply. "He isn't?" He hesitated. "Yes, you can help. I'd like to report a missing person," Blake said. He listened for a moment, then, replied, "He's seventeen and he's my son."

Five

Sheriff Carson Katts arrived fifteen minutes after Blake made the call to the police department. Carson and his wife, Missy, had been friends with Blake and Nichole for years. Carson also coached Keith, who was on the school's football team.

After asking the usual questions, such as height, weight, age, identifying birthmarks, tattoos, etc., Carson started to get personal. "Has Keith had any problems lately?"

Nichole looked over at Blake, not saying anything.

"Well?" Carson asked, waiting for a reply.

"You know Keith. He's not the sort of kid who flies off the handle over nothing. But, Tuesday at dinner he lost it and he stormed out of the house," Blake said.

"What do you mean, he lost it?" Carson asked.

"It's my fault," Nichole told him. "I've been neglecting him and Blake and I have been fighting about Kari and – well, it all came to a head."

"It's not only Nichole. I'm to blame, too. For the past month, Nichole and I have been having some heated discussions regarding Kari and how to handle her situation. It's been over six months since the accident and I think it's time to let her go. Nichole doesn't want to and I understand her point of view. But the odds are that Kari will never wake up again. I'm having money problems. Since Kari's accident, Nichole hasn't worked and it's been hard trying to make ends meet," Blake explained to Carson.

"I can't even imagine what you are going through. I don't know if I could handle a situation like this. I'd be a basket case, by now."

Nichole shook her head in agreement. "Believe me, Carson, there are days that I am."

"So, Keith has had to sit there and listen to you two arguing over dinner every night. Am I right?" Carson asked.

"Pretty much," Blake said.

"I can't say I blame him for running out."

"I know and we're sorry. Anyway, Tuesday night I guess he had heard enough of the same fight over and over again. He said he couldn't listen to it anymore and he left in a huff. But you know it's not like Keith to take off and stay away. I'm really worried, Carson."

"Do you remember what he was wearing when he left?" Carson asked.

"Jeans, and a . . . What color shirt was he wearing, Nichole?"

"It was a white tee. And, he was wearing his Nike's. Gray and white ones," Nichole responded. "I don't think he took a jacket, but he probably had one in his car."

"All right, then. I have a description of the car and the plates. I'll put out an APB as soon as I leave here."

"A what?" Nichole inquired.

"An all-points bulletin," Carson told her.

"Would you like another Coke," Blake asked.

"I'm fine, thanks. What about relatives? Have you checked with them?"

"Yes. We checked with our parents and our siblings. No one has heard from him," Nichole told him.

"Cousins?" Carson asked. "Is he close to any of them?"

"Too young," Blake said. "None of them are in their teens yet."

Carson looked up from his pad and looked at Nichole and Blake. "Do you have a recent picture of Keith? A frontal view is usually the best if you have one."

"I'm sure we do," Nichole replied.

"His graduation picture is a frontal view," Blake reminded her.

"That's right," Nichole agreed. "Let me go get it."

As soon as Nichole left the room, Carson leaned in closer to Blake. "What about drugs, Blake? Is there any possibility that he's into drugs?"

Blake looked surprised. "God, no, Carson. I've never seen anything that would suggest it."

"Have you checked his room to see if any of his clothes are missing? Is there a chance that he came home while you were at work and picked up a few things?"

"I don't know. I haven't checked his room. Nichole might have. She would know more than I would, anyway. She's the one who buys and washes his clothes. I'll have her take a look if she hasn't already."

"Good. Do you know how much cash Keith had on him?"

Blake shook his head no. "No idea. He has a job and he deposits most of his check into his savings account. He does keep out some money for gas and other stuff. I'll check with the bank to see if he's withdrawn any money in the past couple of days."

The two men looked up as Nichole walked into the room carrying a picture of her son. “Will this do?” she asked, as she handed the picture to Carson.”

Carson took a quick look at the picture. “This should do fine. All right, then, I’m outta here. I need to get on this and get the ball rolling.” Carson stood up and headed for the front door. He turned back to Blake and Nichole and said, “I forgot to ask you. Has Keith ever run away? I mean, did he ever get so upset that he took off for a while? Even when he was a little kid?”

“Absolutely not,” Nichole said vehemently.

“So, no history of running off. That’s good.” Carson didn’t say anything for a moment. “I, uh . . .” He hesitated. “I have to ask this, and I think I already know the answer, but . . . “

Blake stared at him. “For God’s sake, man, spit it out.”

“Have either of you ever been violent with Keith?” Carson asked.

“Seriously?” Blake replied.

“I have to ask,” Carson said.

“No. We don’t believe in corporal punishment. I don’t think either one of us has ever hit either one of our kids.”

“Good.”

“That’s it, then?” Blake asked.

“I’ll get the ball rolling and put out a missing person alert. We’ll check with every kid in his class, teachers, friends, and whoever else we can think of. Someone has to know something.”

“Thanks, Carson,” Blake said.

"The worrisome part of this is that Keith turns eighteen in a few months. Hopefully, he'll be home and safe by then, but once he turns eighteen, he's an adult. If we find out he left voluntarily, that will change everything," Carson told Nichole and Blake.

"What do you mean?" Nichole asked.

"If you're an adult and you want to be missing, that's your choice. We would have to call off the search at that time."

"Well, I sure hope to God he's home long before he turns eighteen," Nichole exclaimed.

"We all do," Carson told her. "I'll be in touch."

"Wait," Blake called out. "Is there any further news on the Douglas car?"

"Oh, it's definitely the car that caused the accident. Our problem right now is that we can't find anyone to come forward and say that Hunter was driving that car the night of the accident. His father is vouching for him, saying that Hunter didn't take the car out that night. Of course, that means that someone else in the family would have been driving it. Besides Hunter and his mother and father, they have two other kids that drive. They've lawyered up so we can't question them at this time. Just hang in there, guys. I'm pretty sure that there will be an arrest before long. All it takes is for one person to step up and say something."

"But if you know it was Hunter driving the car. I don't understand why . . ."

"We don't want to get ahead of ourselves, Nichole," Carson said interrupting her. "We need more proof than what we have right now. Sometimes justice moves slower than we like. We really do need to take this one step at a time."

Six

"I'm so sorry that I haven't spent more time with you the past couple of days, Kari. Your dad and I have been spending a lot of time printing flyers and getting them out to as many people as we can. Almost all of the businesses downtown have allowed us to put one or two in their windows. Plus, we've hung them on as many light and telephone poles that we could manage. I can hardly believe how many people have come out to help us. Of course, almost all of our friends and neighbors are helping us hand out the posters, but there are dozens of strangers helping, too. It seriously does renew your faith in how kind people can be."

Nichole glanced over at Kari and sighed, wishing with all her heart that her daughter could hear her. "We used Keith's graduation picture for the posters. You liked that picture, didn't you? I remember you telling him that you thought it made him look 'sooo sexy' and how he blushed. He is such a nice-looking young man, but, then, both of you kids are good-looking. I'm sure he will break many a woman's heart."

Nichole heard her phone ring and reached over to where it was lying next to her on the small couch. She glanced at it to see who was calling, saw it was Blake, and answered the call. "Hi, honey."

"How long are you going to be at the hospital?" Blake asked abruptly.

"Why? Is something wrong?"

"Carson has some news. He'd like to talk to both of us at the same time."

Nichole felt her heart jump a beat, concerned at what news the sheriff might have. "I can leave anytime," she told Blake.

"It's almost three now. How about I ask him to meet us around four?"

"That's fine," Nichole responded. "Where? At our house?"

"Yes. See you then," Blake said and ended the call.

"Well, that was rude," Nichole muttered to herself, as she walked over to Kari's bed and took her hand. "Did you hear that, Kari? Sheriff Katts has some news about Keith. Wouldn't it be wonderful if they have found him?"

Nichole picked up the book that Dr. Campbell had given Kari and opened it to the first chapter. "I have about half an hour before I have to leave. How about I start reading Rebecca to you?"

"What the hell do you mean he was seen in Milwaukee?" Blake yelled.

"Will you please calm down, Blake," Carson asked. "I said we think it is Keith. The person was caught on a security camera at a gas station and we're not sure if it is Keith. We didn't get a good picture of the car this person was driving, so there's no license plate to check. I want you and Nichole to take a good look at this picture. You two, more than anyone else, should be able to tell if it's Keith."

"Please, God, let it be him," Nichole said softly. She held out her hand. "Let me see it."

Carson handed her the picture and waited while she studied it. "I'm not sure. This person is wearing a dark t-shirt. When Keith left, he was wearing a white one." She stared at the picture for a few more moments. "It certainly could be him. What do you think, Blake?" she asked, as she handed him the picture.

"Did you ever check to see if any of his stuff was missing?" Carson asked her.

"Of course. As far as I could tell, everything was accounted for, except for his school jacket which he usually kept in his car."

"I think this is Keith," Blake declared. "Look at the hair. It's just like Keith's. Yes!" Blake exclaimed excitedly. "This is definitely Keith."

"You're sure?" Carson asked.

"Absolutely."

"Nichole, do you agree with Blake?"

"I guess it could be him," she said. "I can't say I'm one hundred percent sure, but it sure looks like Keith. I don't recognize the shirt, though."

"That's not a big deal," Blake said. "Obviously, he bought a new shirt. After all, he only had the clothes he was wearing when he left. He needed a change so he bought a new shirt, that's all."

"Do you have any idea why he would be in Milwaukee?"

Blake and Nichole looked at each other. "I have no idea," Blake said after a few moments. "Nichole, does Keith know anyone in Milwaukee?"

"I don't think . . . Oh, my God, Blake. Jason moved there, didn't he?"

"Who?" Blake responded.

“Jason Krueger. You remember him, don’t you? His parents got divorced a few years ago and shortly after that Jason and his mother moved to Milwaukee.”

“It’s not ringing a bell.”

“He was kicked off the football team for using drugs,” Nichole told him.

Blake looked confused.

“His mother’s name was Kathleen. She was a good-looking woman, blond hair, and a body to die for,” Nichole told him.

Blake thought for a moment. “She was a tall woman, wasn’t she?” he finally said. “I think she used to be a model or something like that.” He grinned. “Oh, yeah. Now I remember her.”

Nichole looked at him and shook her head. “You can’t remember Jason but you remember his mother? Nice, Blake. Really nice.”

“All right, you two. No fighting. Nichole, what can you tell me about Jason? Were he and Keith close?”

“They were pretty good friends in school. Not best friends, but they spent some time together. In fact, when his parents were fighting and things got rough at home, Jason would come over here to hang out. But, when Jason got into trouble over the drug thing at school, Keith pretty much separated himself from him.”

“What drug thing?” Carson asked.

“Jason was caught with drugs in his locker at school. There were enough of them to assume he was selling them to some of his classmates.” She took a deep breath and let it out. “This doesn’t make sense, Carson. Sure, Keith was upset with us, but for him to drive all the way to Milwaukee . . . well, I'm sorry, it just doesn't make sense."

"Regardless, I'm going to assume right now that the picture is of Keith. I'll contact the Milwaukee police and have them check out this Jason Krueger kid and his mother."

"I just pray to God that Keith is there. You have no idea all the scenarios of what could have happened to him that have been running through my brain," Nichole said, starting to tear up.

"Don't even go there, Nichole," Carson told her. "You'll drive yourself crazy."

Seven

"I'm sorry, but the person in that photo wasn't Keith," Sheriff Katts told Blake. He waited for a response. "Blake, are you still there?" Carson asked, raising his voice.

"Yeah, I'm still here," Blake said softly. "Are you sure? I could have sworn that was Keith. Did the Milwaukee cops talk to that Krueger kid and his mom?"

"They did and the kid, Jason, swears he hasn't seen or talked to Keith since he moved to Milwaukee. His mom backed up his story. Sorry."

"But, just because the Kruegers haven't seen him doesn't necessarily mean that isn't Keith in the picture, does it? I mean, he could still be in Milwaukee. Or, maybe he stopped and got gas there and kept going. It could be . . ." Blake stopped talking for a moment. "I'm sorry. It's just that we were praying that Keith would be there with the Kruegers."

"I know. And, you make a good point. I suppose it might be him in that picture. I'll ask the Milwaukee police to keep an eye out for him. Don't worry. We'll keep on looking for him, Blake."

"So, that's it?" Blake asked.

"For now. Sorry, Buddy, that's all I've got right now. You'll let Nichole know?"

"I will. She's going to be devastated, you know," Blake replied.

"I know."

Nichole was in Kari's hospital room, pacing back and forth. "They say that it isn't Keith in that picture," she said. "At least, the police don't think it's him. Jason Krueger and his mom said Keith never came to their house." She stopped pacing for a moment and looked over at her daughter. "God, Kari, what's happening to my life? First, you have a horrible accident and now Keith is missing."

Nichole walked over to the large window and looked out. "It's raining," she said, as a tear ran down her cheek. "I really thought he'd come back home, you know," she said softly. "We should have reported him missing right away, but we waited. We were so sure that Keith would never do anything foolish. Not our kid. Oh, no. Our family was beyond this type of thing."

Nichole sat down on the small couch and put her face in her hands, crying harder now. "What am I going to do, Kari? I can't lose both of you. Come back to me, will you?" she cried out, raising her voice. "Damn it, Kari, wake up. I need . . . "

"Nichole?"

Nichole jumped at the sound of the voice. She turned to see Dr. Campbell standing in the doorway.

"Are you okay, Nichole?" Ben asked her.

Nichole shook her head no.

"Have you had some news about Keith?"

Nichole shook her head no again and continued to cry.

Ben walked over to her, put his arms around her, and hugged her. "It will be okay," he whispered, as Nichole sobbed on his shoulder.

Nichole's body trembled, as she tried to get control of herself. "I'm so sorry," she uttered. "I think I'm about at my breaking point." She pulled back from him and tried to smile.

Ben took the back of his hand and gently caressed Nichole's face.

She looked up at him, confused by his gesture. Suddenly, realizing what was about to happen, she turned and moved away from him. "I'm such a fool," she told him, as she walked towards Kari's bed. "I'm sorry. But sometimes I just need a good cry. I guess this is one of those times," she said.

"Nichole, I truly wish there was more I could do to help you. And, you can cry on my shoulder anytime you want," he told her, looking into her eyes. He smiled at her. "Anytime," he repeated.

"Dr. Campbell, I was wondering . . ."

"Dr. Campbell? That's kind of formal after all these months. What happened to Ben?"

Nichole smiled. "Sorry. Ben, it is."

"So, what were you wondering?" he asked her.

Nichole stared at him. "I forgot," she finally told him. "God, I hate it when that happens," she said. "Oh, well, I guess it couldn't have been important. On the other hand, how is Kari doing today?"

"I checked on her earlier. I wish I could tell you that I see some changes, but I don't."

Nichole shook her head. "I guess that is both good news and bad news. It depends on how you look at it."

Ben shook his head, agreeing with her. "I prefer to call it good news." He looked over at the door. "I guess I better get moving. It's going to be another busy day."

“Thanks, Ben.”

“Are you going to be here all day?” he asked her.

“I don’t think so. I’ve been neglecting Blake with all that’s going on. I decided he deserves a decent meal tonight, so I’m gonna put on my apron, play the good wife, and cook him dinner.”

“He’s a lucky man to have you,” Ben declared.

Nichole looked away, not saying anything.

“Okay, then,” Ben said. “I’ll see you later.”

“Ben?”

“Yes.”

“You have a couple of kids, so let me ask you something.”

“What’s that,” he inquired.

“What would you do if you were me?”

“Do about what?”

“About Kari. Would you let her go if she was your child?”

Ben looked away, obviously uncomfortable with Nichole’s question.

“I can’t answer that, Nichole.”

“Why not?”

“Because Kari isn’t my child; she’s yours. I’m only her doctor and I can’t make decisions like that for someone else's child.

“Then, what would your wife do, if she was me?”

“I can’t answer that, either. My wife died six years ago.”

Nichole looked surprised. “Oh, I’m so sorry. I didn’t know.”

“It’s all right,” Ben said. “This kind of decision is hard.” He smiled. “You know that, of course. As your doctor, I'm here to do the best I can, but when it comes right down to it, the family has to make the final choice."

"But you must have an opinion about Kari. Am I doing the right thing or not?"

"As I told you before, Nichole, miracles can happen. Kari could wake up again. Or, it will never happen."

Nichole smiled. "You, Dr. Campbell, are absolutely useless."

Ben grinned back at her. "And, you, Mrs. Armstrong, are a pain in my ass."

"I am?"

"Most definitely," Ben said, as he walked out of the room "See ya'," he called out.

Nichole watched as he walked down the hall. "Well, that was interesting," she uttered.

Eight

Christmas Eve

Nichole took a few steps back in order to get a better look at the decorated hospital room.

"This was just a waste of time," Blake complained. "Kari doesn't even know it's Christmas."

"How do you know that, Blake? Some doctors think that comatose patients can hear what's going on around them. How do you know she can't hear the Christmas carols playing? I prefer to think she can."

"And, I suppose she knows you brought her gifts, too," Blake said.

"I don't know what she knows, Blake. But, if she wakes up today or tomorrow, I want her to know that it's Christmas and that we haven't forgotten her."

"Seriously, Nichole, this whole thing is stupid. Kari isn't going to wake up and you've got to accept that. It's been seven months since the accident. How much longer are you going to hang on to some fantasy that she's going to wake up? Even if by some miracle, she does wake up, she'll never be the same. The doctors said she would have permanent brain damage. Is that the life you want for her?" Blake turned away and brushed a tear from his eye.

"I'm not having this fight again," Nichole told him. "Especially not on Christmas Eve."

Blake shook his head. "It's time for you to face the truth, that's all." He looked around the room. "I have to say that the room does look nice, though. You did a nice job."

"Thank you."

He glanced over at a little table holding a small Christmas tree. "What's in that package?" he asked, pointing to one of the gifts under the tree.

"I'm not sure," Nichole replied. "The card says it's from Doctor Campbell. It's probably a book."

"That's interesting. Since when do doctors give their patients gifts?"

"I'm sure he does it for all his patients," Nichole said.

"I doubt that very much," Blake declared. "He must have hundreds of patients. I doubt he buys them all gifts."

"Well, maybe Kari is a special patient. After all, he's been her doctor for a long time now."

"Whatever," Blake commented. "It just seems strange, that's all." He turned and walked towards the door.

"Where are you going?" Nichole asked.

"Home."

Nichole stared at him. "But you just got here," she said. "Aren't you going to stay a little longer?"

Blake looked at Nichole, not moving. "Why? What is there to do here?"

"What do you mean why? To be with Kari and me, that's why. What is there for you to do at home? Wouldn't you rather be here with Kari and me?" Nichole inquired.

"I'd rather you came home with me," Blake stated.

Nichole glanced away. "I can't, Blake. I can't leave Kari here by herself on Christmas Eve."

"And, I don't want to stay here any longer. I hate this place and I hate coming here. I hate that Keith is missing and could be dead for all we know. I hate . . ."

"Stop it!" Nichole yelled. "Just stop it, will you?" She looked at Blake, desperation showing on her face. "Please, have you no faith at all?"

Blake stared at her. "I guess not," he said after a few moments. "And, I don't know how you still do."

"Nichole, what are you doing here?"

Nichole looked up and smiled. "So, Jeanne, you're working on Christmas Eve. Why aren't you at home with your family?"

"I always work on Christmas Eve. However, I do have tomorrow off and I'll be spending it with my kids. My daughter is fixing dinner, so I don't have to cook."

"How much longer before your husband gets home?" Nichole asked.

"Three more months before he gets back from Afghanistan. Three long, long months."

"It sounds like you miss him."

"More than I can say," Jeanne said smiling. "What have you got planned?"

"I'll probably spend most of the day here reading to Kari. I enjoy reading to her, even if she might not hear me."

"What about Mr. Armstrong?"

Nichole looked at her and shrugged. "Who knows?"

"It must be so hard for you," Jeanne said. "I don't know how you manage to hold it together."

"I try."

"Well, I've got rounds to make. Can I get you anything?"

"No, thanks. I'm going to head home and pick up a few things. But I'll be back. I'm spending the night with Kari."

Jeanne smiled. "Well, then, I might see you later. I'll drop off a few pillows and a blanket for you."

"Thank you, Jeanne. Merry Christmas."

"Same to you."

Nichole snuggled beneath the blankets, trying to stay warm. She glanced up at the television, decided she'd seen enough Christmas shows, and turned it off.

She closed her eyes, trying not to think of Keith and Kari and the fight she'd just had with Blake. It's all we do these days, she thought. It's just one big fight after another. My marriage is slowly going to hell and the sad part of it all is that I don't care. I'm just so tired of the fighting and worrying about everything.

As she rolled over, trying to get comfortable, she heard the door open. "Jeanne, is that you?" she whispered.

"Sorry, Nichole. I didn't know you were in here," Dr. Campbell said.

Nichole sat up and turned on a little light near the couch. "Ben?" she uttered, surprised to see him in Kari's room this late at night. "What in the world are you doing here? Why aren't you home with your kids?"

"I was. We celebrated a little but they had plans with some friends. You know how teenagers are. Anyway, I didn't want to sit in an empty house all by myself, so I decided to come and check on some of my patients." He looked at her and smiled. "Better yet, what are you doing here?"

"I wanted to be with Kari tonight. I didn't want her to be alone on Christmas Eve. Blake and I had words again, and I miss Keith and everything is so screwed up. I know I should be at home with Blake, but I just . . ." She stopped talking and sighed. "I'm sorry, it seems that all I do is complain when I'm around you."

"Well, you've got a lot to complain about. I just wish there was some way I could help."

Nichole smiled. "I think the only thing that will help is a miracle."

"The room looks nice. Very Christmassy," Ben commented, changing the subject.

"Thanks. Blake thinks . . . Never mind. Thanks for the gift you got Kari."

"Did you open it yet?" Ben asked her.

Nichole looked up at him and shook her head no. "I'm guessing it's another book."

"It is."

"Thank you. Can you stay a few minutes or are you in a rush?"

"I can stay awhile."

Nichole moved the blanket away and made room on the couch. "Come sit here," she said, as she patted the seat alongside her.

Ben hesitated a moment before he sat down next to Nichole. He let out a sigh and sat back. "This is definitely better," he said.

"Ben, I don't know if I say it enough, but I truly want to thank you for everything that you've done for

Kari. And, for me. You've been a great help to me in dealing with all that's going on and I . . ."

Ben leaned towards her and put his hand on the back of her head, slowly pulling her closer to him. "Shh," he said quietly, as he gently kissed her.

Startled, Nichole started to pull away from him, as she looked questioningly into his eyes. "This is wrong, you know," she whispered.

"I know."

Smiling, she wrapped her arms around him and hungrily returned his kiss.

Nine

May – One Year After the Accident

Nichole put the book down and sighed. "I'm sorry, Kari, I just don't feel like reading today. My mind just isn't on it."

"It's a good time to stop, anyway," Betty told Nichole as she entered the hospital room. "It's time to check Kari's vitals and I need to bathe her."

Nichole looked over at Betty and smiled. "You heard me?"

"Good morning and yes, I did."

"I wonder if Kari did." She took her daughter's hand. "I bathed her already," Nichole said.

"All over?" Betty asked.

"Everywhere, but her back. I have trouble turning her with all those tubes."

"No problem," Betty told her. "I'll take care of it."

Nichole watched for a moment as Betty started checking Kari's vitals. She stood up and walked over to the window. "You know, I think I'll take a walk. It's a beautiful day and I need some exercise."

"That's a good idea," Betty replied.

"It's a year today, you know," Nichole said softly.

"What's that?" Betty said, half listening.

"It's been exactly one year since Kari's accident. And, almost six months since Keith disappeared. No one has any idea where Keith is. They stopped looking for him when he turned eighteen."

"Why would they stop?" Betty asked.

"He's an adult now. He left under his own volition, so there was no sign of foul play and no indication of a crime."

"But just because he turned eighteen shouldn't mean that the cops should quit looking for him."

"I know, but that's how the system works, I guess," Nichole declared. "It's stupid. Plus, even though the police are sure they have the car that hit Kari and Logan, no one has been arrested. They can't prove who was driving. Not one person has come forward to help. Everyone knows it was Hunter that was driving but they can't prove it. Sometimes, I wish Kari had died, too. At least Logan's parents haven't had to watch their son slowly fade away."

"Now, Nichole, you don't mean that," Betty said. "Why don't you take that walk now? It will do you good."

"I guess. Thanks for listening to me bitch, Betty."

"Anytime," Betty replied.

Nichole walked out of the hospital, turned left, and headed toward Centennial Park. She had just entered the park when her phone rang. Seeing that it was Blake calling, she debated as to whether she wanted to answer the call. Ever since Blake had moved out of the house, their conversations were mostly arguments. She gave in to curiosity and answered her phone. "What is it now, Blake?" she said abruptly.

"Hello, to you, too," Blake said sarcastically.

"I'm not in the mood," Nichole said. "Why are you calling?"

"Not to fight, that's for sure. Carson called me a few minutes ago."

Nichole's heart skipped a beat. "They found Keith?"

"No. Hunter Douglas is dead."

Suddenly, Nichole's knees went weak.

"Nichole, did you hear what I said?" Blake asked.

"I need to sit down," Nichole said, as she looked around for a bench or something to sit on. Not seeing anything, she simply dropped down onto the grass. "How?" she whispered.

"It looks like he was murdered. Carson didn't have a whole . . ."

"Murdered?" Nichole interrupted. "Oh, my God. Do they know who did it?"

"I don't think so. All I know is that he was found dead in his car on some old county road. Carson didn't give me the details."

"Exactly when was he killed?"

"I don't know. What difference does it make?"

"I don't know. None, I guess. Well, I'm glad he's dead," Nichole exclaimed.

"For God's sake, Nichole, don't let anyone hear you say that."

"Why not? We all know he was responsible for that accident."

"Nichole, you've got to watch what you say. Right now, the police will be looking at everyone who had a reason to want Hunter dead. And, that includes you and me."

"Well, I certainly didn't kill him. How about you?"

"Of course, I didn't kill him. Why would you even ask that?" Blake asked her.

"I'm sorry I said that. Of course, you didn't kill him. It would take balls to do something like that."

Blake hesitated a moment, then cut off the call.

"Blake? Hello, Blake?" Nichole smiled as she realized he had hung up on her. Looks like he just might have one little ball left, she thought.

As she started to stand up, her phone rang again. "Hello."

"Nichole, Carson here. There's been a development and I need to talk to you. Where are you?"

"I know about Hunter. Blake just called me."

"He told you that Hunter is dead?"

"Yes, and I'm sorry to hear it."

"You are? I'm surprised to hear you say that," Carson said.

"I'm sorry that you didn't arrest him a year ago. I'm sorry he won't be spending the rest of his life in prison rotting away one day at a time. I'm sorry . . ."

"All right. I get the picture. Are you at home? I need to talk to you."

"I'm at the hospital."

"I'd rather not talk to you there. How about you come to the station? Let's say in an hour or so?" Carson asked.

"Am I in trouble, Carson? Why do you need to talk to me? Should I call my attorney?"

"It's just routine, Nichole. I'm sure you have nothing to worry about."

"I know I don't have anything to worry about. How about we meet at my house in an hour instead of at the police station?"

"That's fine, too," Carson replied. "I'll see you then."

"Carson?"

"Yes," Carson answered.

"Don't you think it's strange that Hunter was killed exactly one year after he ran Logan's car off the road?"

"Has it been a year already?".

"To the day," Nichole told him.

Ten

Nichole looked over at Carson, who was flipping through the pages of a small notebook. I never realized how good-looking he is, Nichole thought. Too bad he's married. She sighed, starting to become impatient with him.

"Can I get you some coffee," she asked, interrupting Carson's busy work.

Carson looked up from the notebook and glanced over at her. "What? Sorry, I'm about done here."

"Coffee," Nichole said. "Do you want some?"

"No thanks." Carson looked at his watch, noting the time. He wrote something in his notebook, closed it, and smiled. "Sorry. If I don't write it down when I think of it, I have a tendency to forget it."

"So, what is the it you're talking about?"

"Not important. And, I just realized that I'm off duty. How about a beer?" Carson asked.

Nichole smiled. "Really? You're confusing me. Just why are you here?"

"I just have a couple of questions, that's all. If I feel that the conversation is going in the wrong direction, I'll stop. Right now, though, Nichole, I'm here as your friend."

Nichole looked surprised. "That's good to hear. I'll get you that beer. Be right back," she told him as she walked into the kitchen.

"Hunter was . . ." Carson took a sip of his beer. "Let me start over. Where were you between ten last night and two this morning?"

"Am I a suspect, Carson?"

"Not really. I just need to verify where you were when Hunter was murdered."

"He was killed between ten and two?"

"That's as close as the coroner can come right now. We'll have more of an exact time after he completes his autopsy."

"I was where I am most nights. I was with Kari."

"You spent the night in the hospital?" he asked, looking surprised.

"I spend most nights in the hospital with Kari," Nichole told him. "I don't like being in this big house all by myself at night. I don't sleep well and I pace the floors. I'm usually exhausted the next day. I find I can get a few hours of sleep if I'm with Kari."

"It's been rough, hasn't it?" Carson asked.

"You have no idea."

"What about you and Blake? Do you want to talk about it?"

"What's there to talk about? The fact that we can't be in the same room without fighting? He wants to end Kari's life. I don't. He blames me for Keith storming out and disappearing. I blame him. And, the truth of the matter is, we're both to blame for Keith leaving. We drove him away. Plus, I've filed for a divorce and he's filed a countersuit." Nichole sat back in her chair and smirked. "He wants to sell the house. He says he needs the money."

"That's not unusual in a divorce, is it? I mean, don't most of the assets get divided."

"This is Keith's and Kari's house, too, Carson. What if Keith decides to come back home, only to find he hasn't got one to come back to? Or, by some miracle, Kari gets better?"

"You could buy out his share, couldn't you?" Carson inquired.

"I suppose I could get the money from my parents," Nichole said. "I hate to ask them, though. They've already done so much to help out. They have practically been supporting me since Blake moved out."

"God, Nichole, you really do have your hands full."

"And, the best thing, Carson, is now Blake has decided to go to court and get permission to take Kari off of life support. I'm about to have the battle of my life."

"Well, it has been a year since . . ."

"Don't even start," Nichole said, raising her voice.

"Sorry."

"Do you have any suggestions on what I should do? You and Blake are friends. What does he tell you?"

"Honestly, Nichole, I don't see or talk to Blake that often. As far as suggestions go, I wouldn't even begin to know what to advise you. I just hope you have a good attorney."

Nichole smiled. "I do. I have the best."

"Who is it?" Carson asked.

"Andrew Shields."

Carson stared at her. "You're kidding. How the hell did you manage to get him to take you on as a client? Better yet, how the hell can you afford him?"

Nichole laughed. “Oh, he’s not charging me.”

“Don’t tell me you’re sleeping with that old goat,” Carson said, grinning.

“No, Carson, I’m not sleeping with my uncle.”

“Andrew Shields is your uncle?” Carson exclaimed. He sat back in his chair and shook his head. “I don’t believe it. Hell, you don’t have anything to worry about. Blake’s ass is grass.”

“Hopefully. However, I’ve learned never to take anything for granted.”

Carson glanced down at his watch. “I should probably get going.”

Nichole didn’t say anything.

“Oh, what the hell. How about another beer?”

“Well, I was about to leave.”

“I’ll drink it fast,” Carson said, grinning.

“All right but you only have ten minutes, and, then, I’m leaving,” Nichole told him.

“So, you don’t think there’s a chance you and Blake will get back together?”

Nichole glanced over at him and laughed. “You’re kidding, right?”

Carson shrugged. “Just wondering, is all. Missy and I haven’t been getting along lately. We are trying to patch things up, but it’s not going so well.”

“I’m surprised to hear that, Carson. I always thought you two were the perfect couple.”

“Nah. Far from it,” Carson replied. “So, are you seeing anyone?”

Nichole gave him a look. “You mean dating?”

“Yeah.”

Nichole shook her head. "No. And, I'm not about to start. I've got enough on my plate without putting some man on it, too. No, Carson, I think it will be quite some time before that happens." She glanced at her watch. "Your ten minutes are up."

Carson chugged down the rest of the beer in his bottle and stood up. "Thanks for the beer."

"Anytime," Nichole told him.

"Seriously?" Carson asked, grinning.

"Sure. But, call first, will you?"

Eleven

Hunter Douglas was found at six o'clock in the morning, exactly one year after the car accident that had killed Logan Sands and severely injured Kari Armstrong. He was found slumped over the steering wheel of his father's car.

The autopsy determined that the bruises on his body were due to a severe beating. However, the beating was not what had killed him. Hunter also had seven stab wounds in his chest, abdomen, and right thigh. The coroner determined that a stab wound to his thigh cut the femoral artery, causing him to bleed out and die.

Sheriff Katts read through the autopsy again, noting that the coroner had narrowed down the time of Hunter's death to be closer to between eleven and one o'clock in the morning.

He bent over his desk and started writing names on a yellow legal pad. Without any hesitation, he wrote down the names Blake Armstrong, Nichole Armstrong, Rachel Sands, and Simon Sands and, then, stopped writing. He thought for a moment, trying to figure out who else should be added to the list of potential suspects.

Actually, he thought, I could scratch off Nichole, as I know she was at the hospital when Hunter was killed. Besides, for a woman to overpower Hunter and do the damage that was done is almost impossible. Unless she had . . . Katts sat straight up in his chair. "Of course," he muttered to himself. "Unless there was more than one killer."

Katts picked up the phone and called Dr. Corders, the coroner. He waited for the doctor to pick up.

"Corders here," the doctor answered.

"Sal, this is Carson. I have a question for you."

"Well, make it fast. I'm in the middle of opening up the chest of a twenty-two-year-old female. Another damn drug overdose. What a waste."

"Do you think that more than one person could have been involved in Hunter Douglas' murder?"

"I'd say it was most likely more than one person, but I wouldn't rule out just one person."

"Could a woman have done it all by herself?"

Dr. Corders thought for a moment. "I think the Douglas kid would have had to have been out cold for a woman to do it. Remember, this kid was a football player and he was pretty big. I can't see him being overpowered by a woman. Nope, he was either already knocked out or it was more than one person. I didn't find any wounds that would indicate he had been knocked out and no sign of drugs in his system. I'd say he was awake when he was attacked."

"Right. Thanks, Sal."

"Carson, you know that all indications are that he was killed by someone he knew. Being beaten and, then, stabbed usually turns out to be a rage killing. This murder was close up and personal."

"Yeah, I figured that was probably the case. Right now, I'm thinking it was someone looking to get revenge for Kari Armstrong and Logan Sands."

"Logan Sands? I remember him. He was killed in a car accident, wasn't he?

"He was. And, Kari Armstrong has been in a coma ever since.

"That was over a year ago if I remember right. It seems like a long time to wait to get revenge, Carson."

"It does. But who knows what goes through people's minds? Besides, the fact that Douglas was killed exactly one year to the day after that car accident doesn't seem like a coincidence to me."

Over the next three days, Sheriff Katts interviewed Blake Armstrong, Rachel, and Simon Sands. The Sands vouched for each other, telling Katts that they were home in bed sleeping at the time of the murder.

Blake Armstrong insisted that he had nothing to do with Hunter's murder, telling Katts that he also had been home sleeping when Hunter was killed.

"Is there anyone who can back up your alibi?" Katts had asked Blake.

Blake had stared at Katts, not believing what he had just heard. "What the hell, Carson? You of all people should know I would never have killed that kid. If I wanted him dead, I sure as hell wouldn't have waited a year to kill him. Are you seriously telling me that I need an alibi? I thought you knew me better than that. I thought you were my friend."

"It's my job, Blake," Katts had said.

"Well, you can take your job and shove it."

"Come on, Blake. You know that everyone is a suspect right now."

"Really? Well, what about Nichole? Why haven't you dragged her down here and given her the third degree?"

"She has an airtight alibi. You don't."

“What about the Sands? It’s their kid that was killed in that accident. They sure as hell had a reason to kill Hunter.”

“It doesn’t look like they did it either,” Katts replied.

“Well, it sure as hell wasn’t me,” Blake said.

A search of the area where Hunter had been found turned up nothing. Several policemen had been assigned to interview the residents that lived in the area. However, seeing he was found in the country and due to the distance between the houses, it led nowhere.

“I’ve got jack squat,” Katts muttered.

“What’s that, Sheriff?” Deputy Truhouse asked.

“Nothing.” Katts looked over at the Deputy. “What am I missing here, Mikey? I haven’t found one piece of evidence that I can use. No fingerprints on the car, no murder weapon, no witnesses, nothing. I just get this horrible feeling that we’re going to have another case go unsolved if something or someone doesn’t turn up.”

“Another case?” Truhouse asked.

“Yes, another. We never closed the case on Logan Sands and Kari Armstrong.”

“Well, in a way it’s been closed,” Truhouse told him.

“Really? And, how did I do that?”

“You didn’t. But whoever killed Hunter Douglas sure as hell did.”

“What the hell are you talking about?” Katts asked. “We never proved that it was Hunter driving that car.”

“Come on, Sheriff. We all know it was him driving that night. As far as I’m concerned, I’d say the case is closed. Justice has been served.”

Katts stared at Truhouse. "You really feel that way?"

"Well, let's just say I'd put that file on the bottom of the pile and get on with other things."

"Maybe, you're right, Mikey. But I can't do that. One way or the other, I'm going to find out who killed that kid."

"Your choice," Truhouse replied.

"Damn right, it is."

Twelve

"Good morning, Nichole," Dr. Campbell said as he walked into Kari's hospital room.

"Good morning."

"So, how's our girl doing today?"

Nichole shook her head. "No change as far as I can tell." She looked down at her daughter. "Does she look like she's lost more weight? Her face looks thinner to me."

Ben looked at Kari and shrugged his shoulders. "I don't know. She doesn't look any different to me but you're more likely to pick up on something like this. I'll have her weighed. I don't want to see her weight drop anymore. If she has lost a few pounds, we will definitely up her calorie intake."

"Thanks."

Ben finished checking Kari, turned, and looked at Nichole. "Don't you think we should talk about the elephant in the room?"

Nichole smiled. "Not really. I don't think there's anything to talk about. We agreed that what happened on Christmas Eve was a mistake."

"I know we did. You were married then and it was wrong. It's just that when I see you, I feel like I've lost a friend. It's different between us now."

"Ben, I will always consider you my friend. I'd be lying if I said I wasn't attracted to you, but you're Kari's doctor and it just doesn't seem right for you to be anything more than that."

"I'm here for you if you need anything, you know."

"I know," Nichole replied. "I truly appreciate everything . . ."

Dr. Campbell reached out and took Nichole's hand. "I know you do." He looked at her and smiled. "Would it be inappropriate if I asked you to go to dinner with me some night? Just dinner, that's all. As friends. I don't know about you, but I could use a nice meal and some light conversation with a friend."

Nichole frowned, thinking about his invitation. "I don't know if that's a good idea."

"It's just dinner, Nichole. I won't even pick you up if that concerns you. We can meet at the restaurant."

Nichole smiled. "That isn't what concerns me, Ben. What concerns me is that I don't know if I can keep my hands off of you."

Ben, looking surprised, let go of Nichole's hand and took a few steps backward. He stared at her for a moment, then, grinned. "Damn."

"I'm sorry. I shouldn't have said that."

"I'm glad you said that," Ben told her.

Nichole walked to the window and looked outside. "Let me think about it," she said. "I'm not sure that just dinner is even a good idea."

"So, it's a maybe, then?" Ben asked her.

"You mean, that maybe I'll think about it?" Nichole asked, smiling.

"Just think about it, will you?" As Ben walked towards the door, he turned and grinned. "You're still a pain in the ass, you know."

"I know."

"What do you want, now, Blake?" Nichole asked as she answered her phone.

"I just got a call from Pat Wilcox. Have you talked to her today?"

"No. I haven't seen her in a few days. Why?"

"She thinks she saw Keith's car drive past the house early this morning."

Nichole closed her eyes and took a deep breath. "She thinks she saw his car, but she's not sure?"

"She said she was almost positive."

"Why didn't she tell me this morning? She lives right next door, for God's sake."

"I don't know, Nichole. I'm just passing on what she told me."

"Could she see who was driving? Was it Keith? Did she call the police and tell them?"

"Slow down. One question at a time."

"Well?" Nichole responded.

"She couldn't see who was driving, so we don't know if it was Keith. And, no. She didn't call the police."

"Why not. Why wouldn't she call the police, Blake, if she's so sure it was Keith's car?"

"I don't know. Maybe, it's because he's considered an adult now and it's no longer an open investigation. However, I've got a call into Carson and I'm waiting for him to call back. I'm going to ask him if he can put an APB on Keith's car. If he's still in the area, maybe they can find his car."

Nichole didn't say anything.

"Are you still there?" Blake asked.

"Sorry. I'm shaking so bad right now I can hardly talk," she told him. "What can we do? I mean, is there anything we can do to help find him? Oh, my God, Blake. What if he is back in town? He'll come home, won't he?"

"I honestly don't know what's going through his head. He's been gone over six months."

"I know how long he's been gone, Blake," Nichole said abruptly. "I know how many days, how many hours, and how many minutes. You don't have to remind me."

"I've got to go. I'll call you after I hear back from Carson."

"Maybe, I should . . . Blake are you there?" Nichole stared at the screen of her phone, realizing that Blake had ended the call. "What a prick," she uttered softly.

"Who's a prick?"

Nichole jumped and turned to see Betty standing behind her. "You just scared the crap out of me," Nichole said.

"Sorry. So, who are you so upset with?"

"My idiot soon-to-be ex-husband just hung up on me."

Betty stared at Nichole, suddenly concerned about the way she looked. "You're really flushed. Do you feel okay?"

"Not really. My neighbor thinks she saw Keith's car drive past her house this morning but she doesn't know if Keith was driving it or not. I'm not sure how I'm feeling right now, Betty, except helpless. I don't know what to do or expect. If it was Keith, why hasn't he come home?"

"Have you contacted the police?"

"Blake has. He's waiting for a callback. Waiting, waiting, waiting. That's all I've done for the past year. Waiting for Kari to wake up, waiting for Keith to come home. Waiting for this damn divorce and lawsuit to end. I just don't know how much longer . . ." Nichole's eyes filled with tears and she started to cry. "I'm sorry," she said.

Betty walked over to her and put her arms around her. "Nothing to be sorry for. Just let it out, hon. You go right ahead and cry."

As Nichole cried on Betty's shoulder, she didn't see Dr. Campbell standing in the doorway watching her. He hesitated a moment, then turned and continued on down the corridor.

Thirteen

"We've got his car, but Keith wasn't driving it."

"What do you mean, Keith wasn't driving it?" Nichole exclaimed.

"It was Jason Krueger, that kid from Milwaukee."

"What? Why was he driving Keith's car? Did he tell you where Keith is? Is he okay? For God's sake, Carson, do you know anything about my son?" Nichole asked, obviously upset.

Sheriff Carson looked across the table at Nichole, worried that she was about to completely lose it. "Nichole, can you quiet down for a minute? Please, just let me finish telling you what we have so far and then I'll answer your questions," he said, slightly raising his voice. He picked up his cup and took a sip of his coffee, waiting for Nichole to compose herself.

Nichole gave him a dirty look, crossed her arms, and sat back in her chair, glaring at Carson. "You didn't have to yell at me."

"I'm sorry, but you tend to get carried away."

Nichole continued to stare at him but stayed quiet.

Carson stood up and walked over to the kitchen counter and poured himself a fresh cup of coffee. "You do make a good cup of coffee," he commented.

Nichole picked up her cup, finished what was left in it, and handed her cup to Carson.

Carson smiled as he took her cup and refilled it. He handed it back to her and sat back down at the table.

"Thank you," Nichole said, softly.

"You're welcome. Your neighbor, Pat Wilcox, was right when she said she saw Keith's car. I put out an APB, as I said we would, and one of our patrol officers noticed the car parked in front of Wendy's. He parked his squad car and went inside to check to see if Keith was there. Seeing no one that fitted Keith's description, he left and went back to his car. He then parked his car around the corner, where it would be out of view. He waited until he saw a young man leave Wendy's and start to get into the car. He pulled in behind Keith's car, blocking him so he couldn't leave, and approached the young man. The officer asked for some identification and the young man was identified as Jason Krueger, who lives in Milwaukee." He paused to take a drink of coffee.

"That's it?" Nichole asked.

Carson shook his head no. "The officer called to have the car impounded and took Krueger down to the station. At first, Krueger wouldn't talk. However, after a few hours of being questioned, he finally told us that Keith had been staying with him and his mom. He said that Keith had given him permission to use his car." He watched Nichole's reaction to this statement, and realizing that she was about to say something, he held up his hand, stopping her.

"Hold that thought. I'm just about done. Okay?"

Nichole shook her head yes.

"Krueger insists that Keith had not been to his house before the Milwaukee police were there. He told us that Keith showed up the following week. Personally, I think he's lying, but I can't prove it. He told us that Keith has been staying with him and his mom since then. He said Keith insisted that he didn't want you or Blake to know where he was."

"But, why was Jason in town? And, why was he driving by my house?" Nichole blurted out.

Carson grinned. "You almost made it to the end," he said.

"Sorry. Continue, please."

"Keith asked him to get some of his things. Krueger was going to wait until you left the house and then break in. He showed us a list of things that Keith wanted him to take. Mostly clothes, but he wanted his iPod and some of his books and a bunch of other stuff."

Surprised, Nichole sat back in her chair. "You're not serious?"

"I'm sorry, but I am."

"So, Keith's in Milwaukee?"

"According to Krueger, he is."

Nichole studied Carson's face for a moment and frowned. "What else?"

"What do you mean?"

"What else, Carson? What aren't you telling me?"

"I'm not sure if I . . ."

"Just tell me, will you?" Nichole interrupted.

Carson hesitated. "All right, but don't get all excited when I tell you."

"Tell me what?"

"We asked forensics to check out every inch of Keith's car."

"Why would . . ." Nichole suddenly felt sick to her stomach.

"Are you okay?" Carson asked.

"You found something?

Carson looked away, not responding.

What did you find, Carson?"

"We found some blood in the back seat and in the trunk of the car. We haven't tested it yet, so don't jump to conclusions. It could be from anybody. But we are checking to see if it is Keith's blood."

"How much blood?" Nichole asked.

"Enough to be concerned," Carson said. He glanced over at Nichole and noticed that the color had drained out of her face. Realizing she was about to faint, he jumped out of his chair and caught her just as she went limp and started to slide out of her chair.

Nichole's face was wet. She opened her eyes and saw Carson kneeling beside her, holding a dripping wet towel.

"I think you're trying to drown me," she said.

"Ah, there you are. Welcome back."

"What happened?"

"You fainted."

"I did?"

"You did."

"How did I get on the couch?"

"I carried you."

"All by yourself?"

"You're as light as a feather. Do you feel good enough to sit up?"

Nichole started to sit up, changed her mind, and stayed lying down. "I think I need a little help. I'm still a little dizzy."

Carson looked over at her and smiled.

"What?"

"Do you have any idea how beautiful you are?"

Nichole grinned. "Even with a wet head?"

Carson, who was still on his knees, bent over her and ran his fingers through her wet hair. "I mean it, Nichole. I think about you all the time." He put a hand under her head and started to pull her face closer to his.

"What do you think you're doing?" Nichole shouted, trying to push him away.

Carson grabbed her wrists and pinned her down. He brought his mouth close to hers, hesitating for only a second before kissing her.

Knowing that she could not fight him and win. Nichole struggled for only a moment before she went limp.

"I've dreamed about this for years, Nichole," Carson muttered, breathing heavily as he started unbuttoning her blouse.

As he started to caress her breasts, Nichole moaned, her body aching with desire.

"You want it, don't you?" Carson asked, surprised at her response.

"No. Please, Carson, stop."

"Say it. Tell me you want it." Carson said again, as he pulled her skirt up and reached down inside her panties. "Say it, Nichole."

Nichole gasped as his fingers rubbed her.

"You're so wet," Carson exclaimed. "Say you want it, damn you."

"Yes," she moaned. "Oh, God, yes."

Nichole was in her robe, sitting on the couch, her legs tucked under her, drinking a beer. "I have to admit that it was good, but it was wrong. I want you to understand that this was a one-time thing. You're married, Carson. This can never happen again."

Carson shook his head in agreement. "I know. I should say I'm sorry, but I'm not. I enjoyed every minute of it."

"In fact," Nichole continued, "I'm still married, in case you didn't know. My divorce isn't final yet and if this got out Blake could make things rough for me."

"I know."

Nichole looked away. "Keith and I stopped having sex after Kari's accident. This is the first time since . . ." Her voice trailed off as her eyes filled with tears.

"Oh, my God, Nichole. I had no idea. I didn't plan this, believe me. It just kind of happened."

Nichole wiped the tears from her eyes and looked over at him. "And, it will never happen again. Am I clear?"

Carson grinned. "I hear you loud and clear. The only problem is, now that I've made love to you, I want you more than ever."

"Is that what that was? Making love? As far as I'm concerned, that was nothing more than two horny animals satisfying their sexual needs. And, that is not going to happen again. Now get out of here and go find my son."

Carson stood up, walked over to her, and took her hand. "I don't know if I can promise that, Nichole."

"Leave."

Carson bent down to kiss her. "I don't want to leave yet."

"I mean it, Carson," she said, turning her face away.

Still holding her hand, Carson pulled her up off the couch. "Let's go to your bedroom," he said softly.

Nichole pulled her hand away and stared at him. "What is wrong with you? Didn't you hear what I just said?"

"Sure, I did. You said that we had sex like a couple of horny animals and that's all it was. Maybe, that's all it was to you, but . . ."

"No buts about it, Carson. No more."

"One more time, Nichole. That's all I ask. Let me have one more time to hold you in my arms and . . ." Carson looked away, not finishing his thought.

"And, what? What happened wasn't enough for you?"

"It was what it was. Just sex. Just hot-blooded passionate fiery sex and it was great. But, this time . . ."

"Stop, Carson. There isn't going to be a this time."

Ignoring her comment, Carson pulled her close to him and gently kissed her. "This time, Nichole, I want to make love to you."

"Damn you, Carson."

Fourteen

"Do you remember Jason Krueger, Kari? He was in Keith's class and Keith hung around with him until Jason got into trouble." Nichole took her daughter's hand and stroked it. "Anyway, he – Jason – was picked up by the police driving Keith's car. He was in town to break into our house and get some of Keith's things. At least that's what he said."

Nichole let go of Kari's hand and stood up. She walked over to the window and looked down at the sidewalk. From the window, she could see a large parking lot across the street and a beautifully manicured lawn in front of the hospital. "The lawn people here sure do a nice job. The flowers out front are gorgeous. I wish you could see them."

Nichole sighed and walked back to the chair beside Kari's bed and sat down. "I'm worried, Kari. They found blood in Keith's car. They think it might be Keith's blood. That Jason kid told the police that Keith had been staying with him and his mom, but I don't know if I believe that. Anyway, the Milwaukee police are checking to see if Keith is there."

"I'm her father for crying out loud," a man in the hall yelled.

"Please, Mr. Armstrong, quiet down," a woman said.

Nichole turned to see what the commotion was all about and was surprised to see Blake standing in the hallway talking to Betty. She got up and walked to the doorway. "Blake, what are you doing here?"

Blake turned and looked at Nichole. "I should have guessed you'd be here. You're always here being the dutiful mother, aren't you?"

"Betty?" Nichole asked.

"I think he's had a lot to drink. I asked him to leave."

Even though Blake was standing a few feet away from her, Nichole could smell the booze on his breath. She backed away from him, totally disgusted. "You're drunk." she declared. "Is that what it takes for you to come and visit your daughter? Do you really need to get drunk to find the courage to come here?"

"So, what if I've been drinking? I'm celebrating. Anyhow, what the fuck do you care?" Blake muttered. "I have a right to see her."

"Not like this you don't," Nichole told him angrily. "Go home and sober up."

"I'll go home when I'm good and ready and not . . . Oops, I almost fell down," Blake said, laughing, as he staggered up against a wall.

Nichole looked over at Betty. "Security?"

"On their way," Betty replied.

"You think they can get me out of here before I see my daughter? No way. Now move." Blake stumbled towards Nichole and tried to push her out of his way so he could enter Kari's room. "Get out of my way, bitch," he yelled, shoving her back into the room. "I want to say goodbye to my daughter."

Nichole stared at him for a second as his comment sunk in. "What do you mean, say goodbye?"

"The judge ruled today. Did you miss it? Oh, ya, that's right. You weren't there. Too bad, Nichole. You lost. I won." Blake stumbled and reached for the chair by Kari's bed to steady himself. "I guess it's time you said your goodbyes, too."

"No. That's not right. The hearing isn't until next month."

Blake laughed nastily. "It was changed, Nichole. I guess your uncle forgot to tell you." He looked over at the door, saw two security guards, and grinned. "Guess my escorts are here." He took Kari's hand and squeezed it. "Goodbye, Kari. I love you, baby girl. Now, you'll finally be able to rest in peace."

"No," Nichole cried out. She turned and looked at Betty. "Where's Dr. Campbell? Please, find Ben for me."

"There must be something you can do," Nichole pleaded.

"Believe me, Nichole, if there was, I would have done it a year ago."

"He's going to kill her, Ben," Nichole said, as the tears ran down her cheeks. "He said the judge approved his request to have her taken off all life support."

"What happened? Have you talked to your attorney? It doesn't sound right that they changed the hearing date and you weren't notified."

"I've got a call into my uncle to find out what's going on. Maybe he can file an appeal. Or, get the order overturned. If nothing else, we need to drag this out as long as possible."

"If there is anything I can do to help - well, let me know," Ben said.

"What about the sleeping pill thing? Could you give that a try?" Nichole asked.

Ben looked at her and smiled. "You've been doing your homework."

"Of course, I have. I read about how a whole bunch of people that were in comas woke up after being given sleeping pills. Ambien, I think it was. Would that work for Kari?"

"I doubt it, Nichole. The severity of their injuries were not as bad as Kari's. But, you're right. It has brought quite a few people back."

"If Blake gets his way, Kari could be dead in a few days. What's the harm in trying it?"

Ben was quiet, thinking of what to say. "You're right. Kari could be gone in a few days. But she could also continue to live after she's taken off support. There are hundreds of cases where people who were taken off of life support actually came out of their comas."

"So, she might not die right away?"

"Maybe not or maybe she will. I have no way of knowing. She's breathing on her own, so who knows what may happen."

"Will you try the sleeping pills?" Nichole asked, hoping Ben would agree.

"This is something that would have to be approved by the Hospital Board, Nichole. It could take a while."

"We don't have a while, Ben."

"Let's wait until you hear from your uncle before we do anything. Right now, the best thing would be if he can get that damn order put on hold."

Nichole shook her head, agreeing with him.

"Good. Now, how are you doing? You look tired."

"The truth?"

"Of course."

"I'm slowly going mad. At least, that's how I feel most of the time. I'm waiting to hear if that was Keith's blood in his car. I'm dealing with my divorce and this judgment to take Kari off life support. I don't know if my son is alive or dead. I'm not sleeping well and I'm tired and frustrated most of the time." She stopped and took a deep breath. "I'm waiting to hear from my uncle to find out what the hell is going on and . . ." She smiled. "That's enough. Now, aren't you glad you asked?"

Ben reached over and gently stroked her cheek. "You do have your hands full, don't you?"

"I would just love a good night's sleep. I don't know how much longer I can get by on only three or four hours of sleep a night."

"Now, that's something I can help you with. How about I write you a prescription for some sleeping pills?"

Nichole, looking concerned, shook her head no. "I don't think so. I don't like taking pills."

"I'll only write it for a few pills. Try one and see how it works. If you don't like it, don't take it anymore. But, maybe at least you'll get one good night's sleep. What do you say?"

Nichole hesitated for a moment. "I don't know . . . I guess trying one wouldn't hurt. Thanks, Ben."

"One more thing, Nichole."

"Yes?"

"After you get that good night's sleep, maybe we can do that dinner we talked about."

Nichole smiled. "Maybe we can."

Fifteen

Nichole wondered who would possibly be ringing her doorbell this early in the morning. She glanced over at her clock, surprised to see that it was almost ten. She had slept almost twelve hours straight. The sleeping pill had certainly worked.

She threw on her robe as the doorbell rang again. "Hold on. I'm coming," she yelled, as she made her way to the front door. She started to open the door and, then, stopped when she saw that it was Sheriff Katts.

"Morning, Nichole," he said.

"What do you want, Carson?"

"I have some news. May I come in?"

"No, you may not." She held the door halfway open, attempting to block any attempt the Sheriff may have to come into the house.

"It's about Keith, Nichole."

Nichole felt her heart accelerate, fearing what Katts was about to tell her. "What about Keith?" she asked softly. "Did you find him?"

"Are you going to make me stand out here? Just let me in. I'm not going to try anything."

Nichole studied his face for a second and decided he was serious. After checking to be sure her robe was properly closed, she opened the door all the way. "All right. Come on in, but no funny business."

"Of course not," he replied.

"I mean it."

"Can we sit?"

Nichole led him into the living room and gestured toward a chair. "You sit over there."

Carson waited while Nichole sat down on the couch.

Nichole looked over at him. "Well?"

"Some of the blood that was tested was Keith's."

"Oh, God, no," Nichole moaned.

"There's more, Nichole," Katts said.

Nichole stared at Carson. "No. Not more bad news, please. I don't know if I can take it."

"I'm sorry, but you need to know this."

Nichole closed her eyes and took a deep breath. "What is it?"

"Most of the blood we tested was a match to Hunter Douglas. It looks like he may have been killed in Keith's car."

Nichole parked her car in the hospital parking lot and looked up at the window in Kari's room. I'm so tired of coming here day after day, she thought. Maybe Blake is right and I should just let her go. She put her hand on the door handle and was about to exit her car when her phone rang.

She looked at the caller ID. "About damn time," she said to herself. "Uncle Andrew, what the hell is going on," she said loudly, as she answered her phone.

"Nikki, settle down," her uncle told her.

"Settle down? My little girl is about to be taken off life support and you want me to settle down? Where have you been?"

"It was a total mix-up by the courts. I've talked to the judge that handed down that dumb-ass judgment and it's been rescinded. No one is taking Kari off life support at this time."

Nichole started to cry. "Thank you, Uncle Andrew. I've been beside myself with worry. Thank God, that's over."

"Well, it isn't exactly over. We still have our hearing next month. But, until then, you can rest easy. In fact, I have my doubts that any judge is going to take Blake's side regarding this matter. In the meanwhile, don't make yourself sick over this."

"That's easy for you to say."

"Now, what's this I hear about Keith?"

"What exactly did you hear?"

"I understand he might be a person of interest regarding that Douglas kid's murder."

"The police told me that they found blood in Keith's car. Most of it was a match to Hunter Douglas, but some of it was Keith's blood. I know my son, Uncle Andrew, and Keith would never hurt anybody, much less kill someone. If anyone killed Hunter Douglas it was probably Jason Krueger."

"Who is Jason Krueger?' Andrew asked.

"He used to live here and he hung around with Keith for a while. He and his mom moved to Milwaukee a few years ago. Anyway, the police picked him up here in town a few days ago. He was driving Keith's car. He told the police that Keith has been staying with him."

"Do you think that's true?"

"I have no idea. I've reached the point where I don't want to speculate. But, until I hear otherwise, as far as I'm concerned Keith is still alive."

"That's my girl. You must stay positive, Nichole."

"Again, easier to say than do. But I'm trying. Believe me, I'm trying."

"Good girl."

"By the way," Nichole added, "when is my divorce going to be final?

"There are just a few more things to work out. Blake still insists on selling the house."

"No way. I'm keeping the house."

"He is entitled to half of it, Nichole. If you can't buy him out, then you're going to have to sell it."

"I'll see that bastard dead first," Nichole yelled.

"Nichole!"

"Sorry. I didn't mean that. I don't have the money to buy him out, Uncle Andrew. What should I do?"

"You only owe around fifteen thousand on the mortgage. The house is worth around three hundred, give or take a few thousand. Get a loan from your parents for the balance due and pay off the mortgage. Now your house is free and clear of debt.

"Then what?" Nichole asked.

"Then get a home equity loan or refinance and pay off Blake. Not only will that take care of him, but you'll have enough to pay your parents back the money they gave you to pay off the mortgage."

"If I get money from my parents to pay off the mortgage, shouldn't he have to pay back half of it?"

"Absolutely," Andrew told her. "That would be deducted from what he gets. Also, he's responsible for half of whatever expenses you have."

"It all sounds nice, Uncle, but I don't have a job. No bank is going to give me a loan."

“Then, ask your parents to co-sign for you if that’s what it takes.”

“I doubt mom and dad will go for that,” Nichole whined. “Will you talk to mom and dad for me?”

Andrew hesitated.

“Uncle? You still there?”

“I guess I can do that. Keeping you in that house is our last stumbling block. Once that is taken care of, there is nothing left to hold up finalizing the divorce. It’s just a matter of getting Blake to agree to the numbers. We need to get an appraisal on the house, and we need that number to be low.”

“Thanks, Uncle Andrew. I knew you’d figure this out. Love you, bunches.”

“Love you, too, Nikki. I’ll talk to you later.”

“Bye.”

Sixteen

Sheriff Katts pushed his chair away from the table and stood up. "I'll be right back," he told Jason Krueger. "Can I get you anything?"

"Ya got any Coke?"

"I believe so."

"Bring me a couple of those," Jason said.

"I'll bring you one," Katts said, as he walked out of the room.

"How's it going in there?" Deputy Truhouse asked Katts when he walked into the room.

"I'm not getting crap out of him, Mikey," Katts replied. "I'm just surprised he hasn't asked for an attorney."

"Have you placed him under arrest?"

"Not yet. He says Keith let him use the car and, seeing as how it hasn't been reported stolen, I can't get him on that. Even though he says he was planning to break into the Armstrong house to get some of Keith's things, we picked him up before he had a chance to do it. We haven't got him on anything, except the blood in the car and he swears he doesn't know anything about it. Says he didn't even know it was there."

"Yeah, right," Truhouse said, sarcastically.

"Plus, I can't find a connection between him and Hunter Davis. What possible motive would he have to kill him? He wasn't even living here when Kari and Logan had that accident."

"Maybe, he doesn't need a motive. Maybe, he was just helping out a friend. I imagine those two are pretty tight if Keith has been living with him all the while he's been gone.

"So, you think it could be retaliation for what Hunter Douglas did to Kari?"

"It makes sense. Maybe, one night they get to drinking or using drugs and Keith goes off about what Hunter did to his sister. He's upset that it ruined his parents' marriage. He goes on and on about how Hunter has ruined his life and they decide to get revenge. They drive to town, find Hunter, get him in the car, and kill him. After putting his body in the trunk, they drive around for a while trying to decide what to do. Finally, they just dump him back in his car, leaving him for someone to find," Truhouse declared.

"I know it's just speculation, but I've kinda been thinking that, too. But, why wait so long? It's been over a year now."

Truhouse shrugged. "Ya' got me."

"Anyway, I need to pee. The kid wants a Coke. Get one out of the frig, will you?"

"Sure thing." Truhouse watched the Sheriff walk down the hall to the restroom before he got up from his desk to get the Coke. He went into the lunchroom, opened the refrigerator, and looked inside. "No Coke," he mumbled. He grabbed a Pepsi and went back to his desk.

"I hate Pepsi," Jason yelled.

"We're out of Coke. It's this or nothing," Katts told him.

"Fine," Jason said, as he pushed the Pepsi away and slumped down in his chair.

"Now, Jason, let's go over this one more time."

"Why? I've already told you everything I know."

"I know. I just want to make sure we didn't miss anything. Now, tell me again, exactly what day did Keith show up at your house?"

Jason sighed and reached for the Pepsi.

An hour later, Sheriff Katts closed his notebook and sat back in his chair. "And, this is the first time you've been in town since you moved to Milwaukee, right?"

"I told you already. This is the first time I've been back."

"Tell me again why you're here."

"Keith gave me a list of things he wanted from his house and asked me to go get them. He didn't want to come himself because he was afraid someone would recognize him."

"That's right. I remember you saying that."

Jason stared at him.

"Then what happened, Jason?

"That's it. I got into town early this morning, drove by Keith's house to check it out, and went to Wendy's to get something to eat. I've told you this a million times. Now can I leave?"

Katts smiled. "I don't think so, Jason. We found you in possession of a vehicle that belongs to a missing person and we think – actually, we're pretty sure – that Hunter Douglas was killed in that car. We think he was either injured or killed in the back seat of the car and then put in the trunk. And, seeing as how you're the one in possession of the car with his blood in it . . . Well, you can see how we figure you're the one who killed him."

Jason glared at him.

"Did I mention that we found Keith's blood in the car? I guess maybe you killed him, too. What happened? You two get into a fight and you took your big old knife and stabbed him just like you did Hunter? Whatcha do with the knife, Jason?"

"You're nuts if that's what you think. I didn't kill anybody," Jason yelled.

"I think you should know that our forensic guys are checking to see if any of the hair or DNA that was found in the trunk or back seat of the car belongs to you. If it does. . . Well, then it looks like we gotcha."

Jason almost jumped out of his chair. "That doesn't mean jack shit. I didn't have nothing to do with that guy being killed. Keith's been staying with us for months. I've been in his car hundreds of times. My DNA could have gotten in the trunk or back seat any one of those times. This is so much bull . . ." Jason stopped talking and glared at Sheriff Katts.

"Yes? Bull what?"

"I'm done talking to you. You either arrest me or I'm leaving right now."

Sheriff Katts pursed his lips and thought for a moment. "Well, Jason, you forgot option number three. I can hold you for forty-eight hours before I either arrest you or let you walk out of here.

Jason looked shocked. "Hold me on what charges, you prick? I haven't done anything wrong."

"Maybe not," Katts told him. "But you'll be staying with us for a while until we figure this out." Katts walked over to the door and opened it. "Truhouse," he yelled, "come get this slimeball and lock him up.

"I want an attorney," Jason shouted, as Katts walked out of the room.

Sheriff Katts looked up from his desk, as Deputy Truhouse walked into the room.

"Are you sure we aren't allowed to beat up the bad guys?" Truhouse asked Katts.

Katts laughed. "It sounds like he didn't enjoy his trip to the cell?"

"Before this idiot, I don't remember locking anyone up who screamed like him. My ears hurt. I swear to God."

"He's a loud one, alright."

"You've got less than forty-eight hours to either find something or let him go," Truhouse mentioned.

"I know that, Mikey," Katts said. "I'm hoping that a night in jail might make him change his mind and he'll talk. He knows a lot more than he's admitting and he's lying to us."

"You figure?"

"I know it. Sheriff Potts from the MPD called a few minutes ago. He said he sent some men over to Krueger's house to see if Keith is actually staying there." Katts paused, thinking about what he was going to say.

"And?" Truhouse asked, prompting the Sheriff to continue.

"And, Jason's mom verified his story that Keith did show up about a week after the police checked the first time. However, it makes sense that she would say that, seeing as how she had already told them that Keith wasn't staying there. But she also told the MPD that Keith only stayed at her house for a few weeks."

"What?" Truhouse said loudly. "Then, where's Keith been for all these months? And, why is Jason driving his car?" He looked at Katts and shook his head. "Do you think Keith is dead, Sheriff?"

"I honestly don't know what to think. They didn't find a lot of his blood in the car. I think if he'd been killed in that car, we would have found a lot more of his blood. At this point, I think everyone's lying."

"Man, this is all messed up. I've got a really bad feeling about this, Sheriff."

Katts shook his head up and down in agreement. "You and me both, Mikey. You and me both."

Seventeen

September

Nichole put the book down and gazed at her daughter. She looks so small, she thought. She sighed as she reached over and picked up a bottle of water. She took a long swallow and put the bottle back down.

"The leaves are beginning to turn already," she said. "I can't believe that Labor Day is right around the corner." She stood up and stretched. "I'm thinking about getting a job, Kari. I wish I knew how you felt about that. It would mean that I wouldn't be here all the time like I am now. But I'd still be here every night to see you and read to you. Maybe, I could find something part-time. You know, just work mornings or afternoons. That way I'd still be able to spend almost as much time with you as I do now."

Nichole walked over to the window and looked outside. "It looks like rain," she said. "I shouldn't have any problems getting a job. I'm well qualified to do any number of things. Your grandma and grandpa have been wonderful helping out this past year but it's time I started making an effort to contribute."

Nichole walked back over to the chair beside Kari's bed and sat down. "Has your dad been here to see you? Probably not. I seldom hear from him, now that our divorce is final. I heard that he's been dating. In fact, I heard . . ." Nichole laughed. "Sorry, I shouldn't laugh but I heard he's been dating Peggy Robins. I can't imagine what he could see in her. The last time I saw her, she had to tip the scales at over two hundred pounds. Oh, well. To each his own."

"I've gone out to dinner with Dr. Campbell a couple of times. But, just as friends, Kari. He really is a nice man, but I just don't think I could handle being in a relationship right now. Although, I do have my moments when I miss having a man around."

Nichole stared at the ceiling for a few moments. "Have you ever noticed that the ceiling in here could use a cleaning?" Nichole chuckled. "Of course, you haven't. What a dumb thing for me to say."

She stood and started pacing the room. "God, I'm antsy today. Maybe, it's the change in the seasons affecting me. Of course, it also could be the fact that we have to go back to court in a few weeks. I don't know why your father continues to pursue trying to take you off life support. I doubt the judge will rule any differently this time and all your dad is accomplishing is running up his attorney fees. Oh, well."

Nichole looked around the room and suddenly became extremely agitated. I've got to get out of here, she thought. This room – this hospital – is starting to drive me nuts. She looked over at her daughter and felt guilty about her thoughts.

"I think I'll leave now, Kari," she said. She stood in the middle of the room, feeling confused about what to do next.

"Yes, that's a good idea," she said. "I'll go home and check the want ads. Maybe, there's a job listed that I can apply for." She walked over to Kari, bent down, and kissed her. "See you tomorrow. I love you, Kari."

Moments after Nichole left her room, Kari turned her head towards the window and slowly opened her eyes. "Mom?" she whispered, as a tear ran down her cheek. Her eyes closed and within seconds she was pulled back down into her world of darkness.

"I'm telling you, I saw activity on the monitor," Betty told Dr. Campbell.

"Well, I don't see that anything has changed," Dr. Campbell replied. "It had to be a fluke."

Betty hesitated. "Maybe, but something was different – felt different when I went into her room. It looked like she had moved or . . ." She shrugged. "I don't know. Just forget it."

"Had Mrs. Armstrong been in her room before this happened?"

"She had just left a few moments before I noticed the activity."

"I don't know what to say, Betty," Campbell said. "Maybe, her mother moved her or something. Whatever it was, I'm not seeing it now."

Betty sighed. "I know. Me either. I'm sorry to have bothered you, Doctor."

"No. Don't be sorry and it wasn't a bother. If this happens again, I want you to call me immediately."

"Are you sure? It was probably just a little hiccup of the machine."

"I'm sure, Betty."

Nichole stared at the want ads, not really paying attention to them. Suddenly, she threw the paper to the floor and started to cry. "I can't handle this anymore," she mumbled. "It's just too much."

She jumped out of her chair, walked into the bathroom, and opened the medicine chest. She grabbed the bottle that held the sleeping pills and opened it. "Shit!" she yelled when she realized that there was only one pill left in the bottle.

She went back into the living room, grabbed her phone, and call Dr. Campbell. "Answer the phone, damn you," she cried out after a few moments. Finally, after no answer, she ended the call and threw the phone on the floor.

She jumped when the phone rang a few minutes later. She reached down for her phone, checked the caller ID, and smiled. "Ben. How are you?" she answered.

"Nichole, did you just phone me? Is everything okay?"

"Everything is fine and I'm sorry to call you so late."

"It's not that late. What's up?"

"I just noticed that I've only got one sleeping pill left. I was wondering if you could write me a new prescription."

"I was going to ask you about that. Have they helped you? It's been a while since I prescribed them."

"I only use them when I feel that I need some help. But I have to admit that I sleep like a baby when I do take one."

"That's great. I'm glad they have helped you. How about I drop a prescription off for you tomorrow at the hospital? What time will you be there?"

"I'm not really sure." Nichole hesitated for a moment. "Are you at home?"

"No, I'm still at the hospital, but I was just about to leave. Why?"

"I really could use some company. Do you think you could stop by my house? Maybe, we could have a drink and talk for a while."

"I haven't had dinner yet. How about you?"

"No, and I'm starving.

"How about I pick up a pizza?"

"Wonderful. I could go for a few slices."

"Do you like anchovies?"

"I hate them."

"Got it. No anchovies. What do you have to drink? Should I bring some beer or something?"

"I have everything you need right here, Ben."

"Really, Nichole? Everything?"

"Everything."

Nichole rolled over onto her back and sighed.

"You sound satisfied," Ben said, grinning.

"I needed that," Nichole said. "I've been stressed lately and that was quite the stress reliever."

"I'm glad I could be of service, ma'am," Ben joked. "Well, I've got to go," he declared.

"What?" Nichole exclaimed, surprised. "You're leaving? I thought you'd spend the night."

"No can do. I have an early surgery tomorrow and, if I stay here, I doubt I'll get any sleep. Besides, the kids are expecting me." He stood up and pulled on his briefs.

"Your kids aren't babies anymore, Ben. Surely, they can spend one night alone"

"I imagine they can and they have, but not tonight. I need to get up early and it's best if I sleep in my own bed. Maybe, next time I'll stay over."

"But I don't want you to leave. Besides, what makes you so sure there will be a next time?" Nichole asked, starting to get upset.

He glanced over at her and frowned. "I'm sorry, Nichole, but I need to go. There's absolutely no reason for you to get angry."

Nichole reached for the sheet and pulled it up, covering her entire body. "Then, go," she mumbled.

"Stop it, Nichole. you're acting like a child."

Nichole pulled the sheet away from her face and stared at Ben. "Are you still here?" she finally said.

"How much did you have to drink before I got here?" he asked her, concerned about her behavior.

"I'm not drunk if that's what you think," Nichole said softly.

"Well, there sure as hell is something wrong with you," Ben declared. "And, I have to tell you that I really don't care for the way you're acting."

"I'm sorry, Ben," Nichole cried out. She covered her naked body with the sheet and pulled it behind her as she got off the bed. "I am so so sorry. Please, forgive me. It's just that I've been so lonely and it felt so good to have you hold me and I just didn't want to be alone and . . ." She reached out for him. "Please . . ." She looked at him, tears filling her eyes.

Ben reached out and pulled her close. "Of course, I forgive you"

Nichole looked into his eyes and smiled. "I know I was acting like a crazy lady and I . . ."

“Shh,” Ben said, as he gently kissed her.

“This is the first time I’ve had sex since Kari had her accident. It’s been a long time and I just thought . . .”

“My God, Nichole. You should have told me,” Ben interrupted her. “I didn’t know. I had no idea.”

Nichole put her arms around Ben’s neck, letting the sheet fall to the floor. She moved her naked body against him, pulling him close.

“I really have to leave, Nichole.”

“I know. And, you can, right after . . .” She slipped her hand down his briefs, feeling his hardness. She grinned. “Well, what do we have here, Mr. I Have To Leave?”

“Seriously, Nichole, I . . . ”

“Yes?” she teased, as she pulled his briefs further down, totally exposing him. Smiling, she dropped to her knees and looked up at him.

“Nichole, please . . .”

She wet her lips with her tongue and slowly guided him into her mouth.

Groaning with desire, Ben reached down, picked her up, and threw her onto the bed.

Eighteen

September – Labor Day

"It's Labor Day today," Nichole told Kari. "Has Dr. Campbell been in to see you yet?" She walked closer to Kari's bed and bent down. "Do you want to hear a secret?" she whispered in Kari's ear.

Nichole glanced over at the door, making sure no one was listening. "I had sex with Dr. Campbell. And, we did it twice. I told him it was the first time since you had your accident, but I was lying."

Nichole straightened up and smiled. "If I play my cards right, he could be your new daddy. Would you like that, Kari? At least he would visit you every day. That's more than your real father does. He never comes to see you. You know, I never hated your father before we got our divorce. I didn't have any feelings left for him. But, now, I dislike him more and more every day. I imagine it's because of his lack of concern for you and Keith."

As Nichole started to walk away from the bed, Kari's foot jerked. Startled, Nichole turned and looked at her daughter. "What did you just do? Did you move?"

She stared at Kari, wondering if she had imagined it. Kari looked exactly as she had a few moments ago. Nichole let out a small laugh. "Jeez, now I'm seeing things."

"What did you see?" Betty asked as she hurried into the room.

"You heard me?" Nichole asked her, embarrassed.

"Did Kari move?" Betty asked, ignoring her question.

"I thought her leg moved. But, I'm just tired and seeing things, that's all."

"No, I saw something on the monitor. I think there was some movement."

"But, people in a coma don't move," Nichole said.

"No, they usually don't," Betty told her. "I'm calling Dr. Campbell. He should know about this."

"I'm sorry, Betty. Once again, I can't detect any change."

Nichole stared at him. "What do you mean, once again? Are you saying that this isn't the first time this has happened?"

Dr. Campbell and Betty glanced at each other, neither one commenting.

"Ben? Tell me what's going on?" Nichole demanded.

"It's nothing, as far as I can determine. We think we have a messed-up monitor."

"Messed up how?" Nichole asked.

"Every so often it indicates that Kari has moved or that there has been some activity. But, when we check her, nothing has changed. I have a call in to have the monitor checked out."

"Then, I wasn't imagining that I saw her leg move," Nichole exclaimed. "It wasn't a mistake on the monitor, was it Betty? She actually moved." Nichole grabbed Dr. Campbell's hand and held it. "Oh, my God, Ben, she moved. What does this mean? Is she coming out of her coma?"

Dr. Campbell pulled his hand away and rested it on her shoulder. "Sit down," he instructed, as he guided her to a chair. "I want you to listen to me, Nichole. Do not . . . Let me emphasize this. Do not get your hopes up. This can happen. Right now, Kari's vitals haven't changed. Nothing has changed."

"But she moved. I saw it. Betty said she saw it on the monitor, too."

"Nichole, I would give the world to see Kari wake up, but I have to be honest with you. I don't think that is going to happen. At least, not today."

"But . . ."

"Nichole. Absolutely nothing has changed. Do you understand?"

Nichole shook her head yes. "She's not going to wake up today," she said softly.

"I'd like to give you something to help you relax a little. Would you be agreeable to that?"

Nichole looked up at him. "You mean like a tranquilizer?"

"Just for a couple of days. Would that be okay?"

"She's never going to wake up, is she? All these months that she's been lying here, she hasn't heard the books I've read to her or the stories I tell her. She hasn't eaten real food in over a year and a half. The only thing she can do is breathe on her own. What kind of a life have I subjected her to? Blake was right, wasn't he? I should have let her go a long time ago," Nichole said, as the tears ran down her cheeks. "My God, what have I done?"

"Betty, would you get some Vistaril for Mrs. Armstrong?"

"Right away, Dr. Campbell."

"What's that for?" Nichole asked.

"It will calm you down, Nichole. I only want you to take it today and tomorrow."

"I'm not crazy, you know."

Dr. Campbell smiled. "I know, but you are having a rough time right now. This will help you relax."

Nichole wiped her tears away and shook her head. "If you think it's best, Ben."

"I do, Nichole. Trust me."

Nichole stared at him.

"What?" Ben asked her.

"I know something else that will calm me down, Ben," she whispered, reaching for his hand.

Ben laughed nervously, as he backed away from her. "Let's try the medicine first, shall we?"

Dr. Campbell left Kari's room and walked down the hall to the nurse's station. He looked around, saw Betty, and motioned for her to join him.

"What can I do for you, Doctor," she asked.

Dr. Campbell checked to see if anyone was within earshot. Noticing two nurses standing fairly close to him, he took Betty's arm and steered her down the hallway.

"Where are we going?" Betty asked, starting to feel uncomfortable.

"Here is good," Campbell said, stopping in the middle of the hallway. "I need to talk to you about Mrs. Armstrong."

"What about her?" Betty asked.

"You see her every day, right?"

"Usually. Why?"

"Has she been acting different lately?"

"Different, how?" Betty inquired.

"Acting strangely. Slipping into periods of time when she acts like she isn't sure what's going on or, maybe, being more emotional. I'm not really sure, Betty, but she seems different to me. I'm beginning to worry about her mental state."

Betty looked up at him, surprised at his questions. "First off, she's always been emotional. My God, look what she's been through in the last year and a half. I'm surprised she isn't in a loony bin."

"Betty, we don't use that phrase."

"Oh, pooh. You know what I mean." Betty thought for a moment. "You may be right, though. She seems to be talking to herself a lot more. And . . ."

"And, what?"

"She can't sit still. She used to sit by Kari's bed for hours, reading to her. Now, she only reads to her for a few minutes at a time. She paces. A lot. But, really, Dr. Campbell. She's here day after day, watching and waiting for Kari to . . ."

"To?"

"Either wake up or die. And, on top of that, she is doing the same thing with Keith, her son. Waiting for news that he's either still alive or dead. I'd say, with what she's been through and going through, she's about as sane as you can expect."

"I guess you're probably right. But, keep an eye on her, will you?"

"You care about her, don't you?" Betty asked, smiling.

Dr. Campbell returned her smile. "I do and I'm extremely concerned about her well-being."

“Well, don’t you worry. I’ll keep an eye on her. But, she’s a strong lady. I don’t think there’s anything to worry about.”

Nineteen

November

Nichole looked up from the book she was reading and watched Ben walk into the room.

"Morning, Nichole. You're here early today."

"I have an appointment and I wanted to see Kari before I went."

"Anything important?" Ben asked.

"Just a doctor's appointment," Nichole told him. "I'm seeing Dr. Hazelton this morning."

"Mabel or Gus?"

"Mabel," Nichole responded.

"Nothing serious, I hope," Ben said.

"I hope not, too."

"So, how's Kari this morning?"

Nichole gave him a dirty look.

"Did I say something wrong," he asked her.

"Why do you even ask that question?" she asked, raising her voice. "It's pointless. You know that nothing ever changes. She's always the same. Day in and day out."

"Nichole, I didn't mean to upset you. Perhaps, it would be better if I left and checked Kari a little later."

"Do whatever you want, Ben." She picked up the book she had been reading to Kari and turned to the last page she had read. "Let's see, now. Oh, here we are. '*Melody didn't care for the color of the dress that her mother wanted . . .*"

"I get it, Nichole," Ben interrupted. "You're still upset with me. It's been almost two months and I don't know how else to apologize. I'm sorry."

Nichole glared at him. "I'm sorry, too. I'm sorry that I was nothing more than a one-night stand to you. I'm sorry I ever let you into my bed, Ben. Big mistake."

"I told you that I wasn't looking for a long-term relationship, Nichole."

"Oh, you sure did. Unfortunately, you waited until after you had screwed me."

Ben looked at her and shrugged. "What more can I say? Would you be more comfortable with a different doctor for Kari? There are quite a few good ones I could recommend."

Nichole stared at him, not believing what he had just suggested. "Well, well, well. I never expected to hear that from you, Ben. You want out of my life completely, is that it?" Nichole laughed. "I'm afraid that isn't going to happen. Ever!"

Ben looked confused. "Nichole, I'm worried about you. Your emotions seem to be all over the place. Maybe, you should find someone you can talk to."

"Do you mean that you think I should see a shrink?" Nichole looked away. "You might be right," she said softly. "I have been holding a lot in lately and I don't have anyone to talk to. I used to talk to you. Remember when we would go out for dinner and I would unload all my problems on you? You were my sounding board there for a while, Ben. I kinda miss that."

He stood there, hesitating.

"Cat got your tongue, Ben?" Nichole asked.

"I've said I'm sorry and I mean it. I've got to get going. I've got rounds to make. I'll see you later."

"What are you doing for Thanksgiving?" Nichole asked him, as he started to leave the room. "Would you like to come over and spend it with me?"

Ben stopped in the doorway, wondering what was going on. "I'm sorry," he finally said, "but the kids and I plan on going up north to my parents' home for the weekend."

"How nice for you." Nichole turned her back on him and continued to read to Kari.

Ben stared at her for a moment. He knew he should say something, but felt it would only open another can of worms and he was tired of arguing with her. "I hope everything goes okay at your doctor's appointment. Let me know how it goes," he said, as he walked out of the room.

Feeling sick to her stomach and knowing she was about to vomit again, Nichole looked back at the door to make sure that Ben had left the room. She only hesitated for a second before she shot out of her chair and made a mad dash to the bathroom.

"Are you okay, Nichole?" Betty asked.

Nichole jumped. "You have to stop sneaking up on me like that," she said angrily. "You scared the b'jesus out of me." She grabbed a towel and wiped off her mouth.

"I'm sorry. I came in to check on Kari and I heard you being sick. Is there anything I can get you?"

"I'm sorry I yelled," Nichole said. "I'm fine. I think I have a little touch of the flu or maybe it was something I ate. Whatever it is, my stomach is a little touchy this morning."

"I can get you some ginger ale if you think that would help."

"No thanks. I'll be fine. In fact, I'm seeing Dr. Hazelton this morning." Nichole glanced at her watch. "I better get moving or I'm going to be late for my appointment."

"I didn't know your internist was Dr. Hazelton. He's mine, too. Don't you just love him?" Betty inquired.

Nichole grabbed her purse and headed for the door. "I'm not seeing him. My appointment is with Dr. Mabel Hazelton. See ya'," Nichole said, as she hurried out of the room.

"See you, too," Betty called out. It only took a moment before it hit her. "Well, I'll be a monkey's uncle," she said. "It looks like Mrs. Armstrong might have gone and got herself pregnant. I wonder who the daddy is."

As Betty clipped a pulse oximeter onto Kari's finger, she sighed. "It isn't as if your mama hasn't got enough problems. I sure hope I'm wrong about this one, Kari girl."

Twenty

Sheriff Katts slammed the phone down and swore.

Deputy Truhouse looked up from his desk. "Bad news?" he asked Katts.

"That damn Krueger kid didn't appear for his hearing yesterday. It looks like he jumped bail. The judge has issued a bench warrant for his arrest. I knew this might happen. I don't know what the judge was thinking when he set his bail at only $25,000.00. He should have known he'd be a flight risk."

"Yeah, but on the other hand, Sheriff, they only arrested him for obstruction and having a little too much pot in his possession. Neither one is that serious."

"I know. But I was hoping he wouldn't let the kid bond out. If he was sitting in county jail waiting for his trial, I'd know where he is. Now, he could be anywhere and I may never solve the Douglas case. I just know that kid had something to do with it."

"I guess," Deputy Truhouse agreed, "but knowing it and proving it are two different things."

"Where do you think Keith is?" Katts asked.

Truhouse shrugged. "What do you think?"

Katts pursed his lips for a second. "I think he's dead, Mikey. I'm just not sure who killed him."

Truhouse stared at him. 'You think Krueger killed him, don't you?"

"Perhaps. Or, it might have been Hunter Douglas. I think Keith and Jason got Douglas in the back of that car and Keith and Hunter got into it. We found blood from both of them in the car. Maybe, they killed each other. Hell, I don't know," he exclaimed frustrated.

"But only Hunter's blood was in the trunk," Truhouse reminded him.

"I just wish we would find Keith. Alive or dead. I don't give a tinker's damn at this point. It's hell not knowing if we're chasing a ghost."

"Isn't your mom going to be pissed?" Keith asked Jason.

"Why would she be pissed?"

"Are you kidding? You just cost her $2,500.00 by not showing up for court."

"She won't care. Hell, that's a drop in the bucket. My mom has more money than she knows what to do with," Jason told him. He glanced around the area, concerned that they would be seen by some nervous neighbor who would call the cops. "We really have to get out of here, Keith."

"We will, as soon as I get my stuff."

"Why is your mom still at home? I thought you said she goes to the hospital every morning."

"She does – or did," Keith replied. "Hell, how do I know what she's doing these days?" He stared out of the car window for a few moments. "It's cold in here. How about we turn on the heat?"

"No way, man. Do you know how suspicious that would look? Two guys sitting in a running car, staring out the windows? Not a good look, man. Someone would be sure to call . . ."

"Hold on. The garage door is opening," Keith interrupted. "It looks like she's leaving."

"About friggin' time," Jason said.

Keith watched as his mother pulled out of the garage and drove away. "She's gone."

"Okay. Here's what we're going to do. I'll drive around the block so we can check to make sure everything is okay. Then, I'll pull into the driveway. You get in and out as fast as possible. I'll keep the car running so . . ."

"No," Keith said. "That would look suspicious. Turn the car off. I'm not going to be in there that long."

Nichole had only gone about half a mile before she realized that she had forgotten her phone. "I swear, I'd lose my head if it wasn't attached," she muttered. As she started to turn the corner to go back to her house, she felt an impact on the back right side of her car.

"What the hell?" she yelled, as she hit the brakes and stopped her car.

"Are you okay?"

Nichole turned and saw her neighbor, Pat Wilcox, walking towards her. She closed her eyes and took a deep breath, trying to keep her cool. She opened her car door and got out. "I'm fine. What happened, Pat?"

"You turned right in front of me. I couldn't stop in time. Anyway, I don't see much damage."

"I'm sorry. I didn't see you." Nichole walked to the back of her car and took a look. "Shit." She bent down and rubbed the car where it had been hit. "There's a dent and a few scratches."

"My bumper has a few marks, but it's not that bad," Pat told her. "I suppose we should call the police or somebody."

"I guess," Nichole said. "Who's your insurance company?"

"Allstate."

"Mine, too," Nichole told her.

"You know, Nichole, I wouldn't object to overlooking this if you want. I don't need the hassle of dealing with insurance companies right now."

Nichole smiled. "Are you sure?"

"I'm sure. This old car has so many dings on it a couple more won't make a difference. Besides, you've got enough to handle right now. Let's forget this ever happened."

"Thanks, Pat. And, I'm sorry. I guess I wasn't paying attention."

"Hey, it happens to the best of us."

"We're good, then?" Nichole asked. "I really should get going."

"We're good," Pat said, hugging her. "You take care now."

Nichole pulled her car over to the side of the street and stopped. "What the hell?" she uttered, noticing a car backing out of her driveway.

She stared at it for a moment before she realized that Keith was sitting in the passenger seat. "Keith!" she yelled. "Wait!"

She threw her car into park and jumped out. "Keith, wait! Stop!" she screamed as she waved her arms, hoping he would see her. She watched as the car sped off down the street. Within seconds it was out of her sight.

"Noo!" she wailed, as she fell to her knees, sobbing.

Sheriff Katts made himself comfortable at Nichole's kitchen table, nursing his fifth cup of coffee that morning. He turned as Nichole walked into the room. "Well?" he inquired.

"It looks like he took almost everything that was his. His winter jackets from the hall closet are gone. So are all of his games – you know, that X-box stuff – and his sports stuff. He basically cleaned out his room." Nichole sat down at the table and sighed. "Why, Carson? After all this time, why now?"

"Nichole, aren't you overlooking the good news here?"

Nichole looked confused. "Good news? My son sees me and won't even stop and talk to me. What's good about that?"

"Nichole, Keith is alive. At least now we know he hasn't been murdered or lying in a ditch somewhere. He's alive."

"You're right. My God, I'm so concerned about him taking his stuff I didn't even consider that. What is wrong with me?" She looked over at Carson and smiled. "My son isn't dead. That is wonderful news."

"However," Carson declared," we may have another problem."

Nichole frowned. "You just couldn't let me enjoy this moment, could you? Now what?"

"Could you tell if the driver of the car was Jason Krueger?"

"Jason?" She thought for a moment. "I honestly don't know. I didn't see the driver's face. I guess it could have been him, but I couldn't swear to it. Why?"

"Jason didn't appear at his hearing yesterday. There's a warrant out for his arrest. If Keith is helping him, he could be in big trouble."

"Oh, crap," Nichole mumbled. "Does it ever end?"

"Can you give me a description of the car they were in?" Carson asked. "I need you to tell me everything you remember."

"Can I do it later? I need to get to the hospital to see Kari."

"Kari's not going anywhere. I want you to do this now, while it's still fresh in your mind." Carson pulled a pad of paper and a pen out of his pocket and looked over at her. "Go."

Twenty-one

"You'll never believe what happened today," Nichole exclaimed as she hurried into Kari's room. "First of all, Pat Wilcox hit me with her car. Well, not me. I meant that she hit my car. It was my fault, though. I was going back home to get my phone – which I had forgotten - and I wasn't paying attention and she hit me. Then, I saw a car backing out of my driveway. It was Keith in the car, Kari! Can you believe it? I yelled for them to stop, but they just kept on going. Sheriff Katts thinks it might have been Jason Krueger driving the car."

Nichole took a deep breath and let it out.

"You remember Jason, don't you? Anyway, the Sheriff told me that Jason skipped out on his bail and now there's a warrant out for his arrest. And, Keith could be in trouble for being with him."

Nichole opened her purse and took out her lipstick. She walked into the bathroom and looked in the mirror. "He took most of his stuff – I mean Keith. Your brother pretty much emptied his room. There, that's better," she declared, as she applied fresh lipstick.

"Grandma and Grandpa Armstrong will be here tomorrow," Nichole informed Kari, as she walked over to her bed and sat down next to her. "I'm looking forward to seeing them. Of course, we'll spend most of the day here with you. The hospital cafeteria will have turkey and all the fixings, so we'll eat there tomorrow. I was going to cook, but Grandma said not to bother. So, we'll all have a happy hospital Thanksgiving."

Nichole picked up a book that was lying on the nightstand and studied it. "Where did this come from? Is this from Dr. Campbell? I'm going to have to tell him to stop buying you books. I don't need his damn charity," Nichole told her daughter, getting upset.

Nichole got off her chair and walked to the door. "I'm going to get some coffee, Honey. I'll be right back."

Nichole stopped in the hallway and looked around. She hesitated a moment and then walked down the hallway to the nurse's station. A woman she did not recognize was sitting at the desk.

"Is Betty here?" Nichole asked, trying to see the nurse's name tag.

"Sorry, but she's not working today. Can I help you with something?"

"You're new here, aren't you?" Nichole asked. "I'm Nichole Armstrong. I'm Kari's mother."

The woman smiled. "Ah, yes. It's nice to meet you, Mrs. Armstrong. I'm so sorry about your daughter. I'm Marjorie Kettlebaum, but everybody calls me Marg."

"And, please call me Nichole. Has Dr. Campbell made his rounds yet, Marg?"

"He has. I believe he's gone for the day. Can I help you with something?"

Nichole smiled. "No, thanks. It can wait." She turned and stared at Kari's room, hesitating.

"Nichole? Are you all right?"

Nichole, looking slightly confused, closed her eyes for a second and, then, looked at Marg. "Sorry, my mind wandered for a moment. I'm fine. I'll be back in a few minutes. I'm going to get some coffee. You're very pretty, you know."

“Thank you,” Marg said. She watched Nichole as she hurried down the hall towards the elevator. “That was weird,” she mumbled to herself. She continued to watch Nichole until she got into the elevator.

“I guess I’ll be going now,” Nichole said. “I want to pick up a few things at the store. I’m not exactly sure what time we’ll be here tomorrow morning. Your grandparents are looking forward to seeing you. Although, I don’t see why they are so excited. Except for it being Thanksgiving, tomorrow is no different from any other day they come to visit you.”

“How’s our girl doing today?”

Nichole turned, surprised to see Blake standing in the doorway. “What are you doing here?” she asked abruptly. “You’re not welcome here, Blake.”

“I may not see her every day like you do, Nichole, but I’m still her father. I have every right to visit her.”

“Why? You’re doing everything you can to kill her.”

Blake took a few steps into the room and stopped. “You get meaner every day, don’t you? Well, I didn’t come here to fight with you.” He walked over to Kari’s bed and gazed down at her. Shaking his head in disgust, he turned and stared at Nichole. “How much longer, Nichole?”

“How much longer what?” She retorted, knowing exactly what he meant.

“How much longer are you going to make Kari suffer? When was the last time you took a good look at your daughter, Nichole? Look at her! She’s wasting away to nothing. Or, maybe you don’t see it even though you come here every day. Maybe, you're too busy playing the martyr and feeling sorry for yourself. Poor little Nichole."

"Shut the fuck up, Blake," Nichole yelled. "I don't need your shit!"

"If you two don't stop it right now, I'll have security kick you both out."

Nichole and Blake looked over and saw Marg standing in the room.

"This is totally unacceptable. There are other patients on this floor, you know. One of you is going to have to leave right now or . . ."

"Well, I'm not . . ." Nichole interrupted.

"Enough!" Marg said loudly. "And, I think it should be you, Mrs. Armstrong. You've been here long enough today."

"I can't leave him alone with Kari," Nichole said. "I don't trust him."

Blake held up his hands, indicating he had had enough. "I can't believe you just said that." He looked at Marg and shook his head. "Don't worry. I'm leaving. There's no winning with this one." He bent down and kissed Kari on her forehead. "I love you, baby," he whispered.

"Sure, you do," Nichole said. "That's why you want to kill her."

Blake stared at her. "You're right. I love her so much that I want to put her out of her misery. That's more than you can say."

"I said enough!" Marg exclaimed. "Both of you - out of here. Now!"

Nichole hesitated a moment, then grabbed her purse and walked out of the room.

"Mr. Armstrong?"

"I'm leaving," Blake told Marg. As he reached the door, he turned to take one last look at his daughter. "What the . . .?" he exclaimed.

Marg turned to see what he was staring at. "What?"

"Look. There's a tear running down Kari's cheek."

Twenty-two

November - Thanksgiving Day

"I didn't want to say anything in front of Kari, but it looks like she . . ." She hesitated.

"Looks like she what, dear?" her mother, Gloria, prompted.

"I think she might be getting ready to wake up. Isn't that wonderful news?"

Nichole's mother glanced over at her husband, looking slightly confused. "I don't understand, Nichole. I was under the impression that a person in a coma just wakes up. I didn't know there were stages that they went through."

Nichole stared at her mother. "I can't believe you didn't know that, Mom." She looked at her father. "You knew that. Right, Dad?"

"What did you mean you didn't want to say anything in front of Kari? Do you still think she can hear you talking? I thought you had put that nonsense behind you, Nichole," her father replied, ignoring her question.

"It's been proven, Dad. People who have been in comas and wake up say they heard people talking."

"Hogwash," her father replied. "They only say what they think people want to hear." He glanced over at his daughter, noticing that her face was turning red. "You're upset. I'm sorry, Nichole. I didn't mean to upset you. I just don't believe it, that's all."

Nichole's bottom lip started to quiver, as she fought to hold back her tears.

"That's enough, Roger," Gloria said sternly. "It's Thanksgiving and you're getting our little girl all upset. Let's just enjoy our dinner, shall we?"

"How often does Blake visit Kari?" Roger asked his daughter, attempting to change the subject.

Nichole's head jerked up and she glared at her father.

Gloria shook her head. "Why would you bring him up? I don't think that's a topic that Nichole cares to discuss." She glanced over at Nichole. "Is it, honey?"

"No, Mom," Nichole answered softly.

Roger threw his fork down on his plate and sat back. "Well, what the hell can I talk about? Perhaps next time we get together you can give me a list of subjects that aren't taboo."

"I wonder what desserts they have here today," Gloria commented. "I hope there's pumpkin pie. I just love pumpkin pie."

"I'm sure they must have some," Roger said. "After all, what's Thanksgiving without pumpkin pie?"

Suddenly, Nichole pushed her plate away and leaned back in her chair. "I can't eat this," she declared.

"Is there something wrong with your food," her father asked her.

"The food is fine, Dad. It's just when I look at all this food – well, all I can think about is Kari who hasn't had a morsel of real food for a year and a half. Every time I close my eyes, I see feeding tubes coming out of her stomach," she said, raising her voice. "I'm gonna do it, Mother. I have to do it for Kari's sake."

"Nichole, please quiet down. People are looking at us," her mother said.

"Oh, screw these people."

"That's enough, Nichole," Gloria said.

"You have to do what?" her father asked her.

"What do you think? It's time to turn off her life support and see what happens. That's what. I can't take this any longer and Kari shouldn't have to either."

"Nichole, look at me," Roger said.

"Why?"

"Because you need to hear this, that's why. Now you listen and you listen good. I can understand how you are feeling. You're tired and you've had enough. Well, get untired, because you haven't been fighting to keep your daughter alive for no reason. She is going to come back to us, Nichole. I truly believe that. Plus, you are not going to let Blake win. You just need to make some changes in your life. It's time you get yourself a job and a life. You are going to stop spending ten hours a day here in this hospital, looking at your daughter. Maybe, she knows you're here and maybe she doesn't. But, one thing I know for sure, Nichole, is that you are not going to take Kari off life support. Do you hear me?"

Nichole shook her head yes.

"Say it."

"Yes, Dad, I hear you."

"Good. Now I'd like to finish my dinner and have some pumpkin pie."

"I'm sorry, Dad, it's just . . ."

Gloria glanced over at Nichole and shook her head, indicating she should be quiet. "I do believe I saw some bread pudding up there. I might have some of that. What about you, Nichole? Pudding or pie for you?"

Nichole stared at her mother.

"Well, what will it be?"

"I'm not sure if I want either one. I'm not that hungry."

"But you've barely touched your food," Gloria commented. "At least eat some of your turkey. It's very good."

Nichole sighed, jabbed a piece of turkey with her fork, and put it in her mouth. "Hmm," she muttered.

"That's my good girl," Gloria said. She looked over at her husband who was getting up from the table. "Would you mind bringing me some of that pudding, dear?"

"Do you really have to leave already?" Nichole asked her parents.

Roger, who was helping Gloria with her coat, smiled. "We've got another stop to make," he told her.

"But you just got here. I don't want you to leave," Nichole whined.

"We've been here since eleven, Nichole. It's almost four o'clock and we're already running late."

Nichole gave her parents a dirty look and sat down beside Kari. She picked up a book and opened it. "So, Kari, do you remember where we left off? Ah, here we are." She started reading to her daughter, totally ignoring her parents.

"Nichole?" her mother said, trying to get her attention. "Aren't you going to say goodbye?"

Nichole glanced up, looking surprised. "Are you still here? I thought you had to leave."

Her father stared at her for a moment. "Come on, Mother, let's go. Your daughter is having one of her moods."

Nichole smiled. “Bye, now. Thanks for coming.” She smiled as she watched her mother follow her father out of the room. “Thank God, they’re gone. I thought they’d never leave,” she said to Kari. “Now, where were we?”

Twenty-three

"Did you have a nice Thanksgiving?" Dr. Campbell asked Betty.

"It was okay. They needed some extra help here, so I volunteered to work. I like making the extra money, especially with Christmas being right around the corner."

"Well, I hope you at least had some turkey."

"I did. After I was done with my shift, I stopped by my sister's for a snack. She's a great cook."

"Anything interesting happening here today?" Dr. Campbell inquired.

Betty looked up at him and hesitated before saying anything.

"What is it?" Campbell asked, looking concerned.

"Do you have a few minutes? There's something I'd like to talk to you about."

"Of course," Campbell replied. He waited for Betty to say something.

"In private, if you don't mind," she finally said.

"All right. There's an empty room down the hall. Let's go there."

Dr. Campbell waited until Betty shut the door. "What is it, Betty?"

"It's Mrs. Armstrong, Doctor," Betty stated. "She's been acting strangely for quite a while now. I mean more than usual," she added smiling, as she noted that Campbell was about to say something.

He grinned. "Go on."

"She's so emotional at times, it scares me. Sometimes she acts confused like she's not sure where she is or what is going on. And, I've heard her vomiting on more than one occasion."

Dr. Campbell stared at her, obviously concerned about what he was hearing. "Throwing up?"

Betty shook her head yes. "I've heard her in Kari's bathroom throwing up. Plus, I know she saw her ob/gyn not long ago. Dr. Campbell, I may be wrong, but I think Mrs. Armstrong is pregnant."

Dr. Campbell was quiet, thinking about how to react to this news. "I have noticed that she is acting differently lately," he finally said. "But, pregnant, Betty? I don't know. Perhaps. Anything is possible, I guess. But, pregnant?" he exclaimed loudly.

"I know. I mean, like, how could this happen? I didn't even know she was seeing someone."

Dr. Campbell reached for a chair, pulled it close, and sat down. "How long did you say she's been acting differently?"

"I figure a couple of months now," Betty replied.

"Good God," he said softly.

"I'm sorry. What did you say?"

He stood up and walked to the door. "As you said, Betty, you could be wrong. I'll try to have a talk with her and see if I can find out what's going on."

"Try?"

"She hasn't been the easiest person to talk to lately. I figured something was bothering her, but I never would have guessed that she might be pregnant."

"I hope I wasn't out of place by saying something to you about this," Betty said. "But I am worried and I know you care for her."

"Not at all. I'm glad you did. She has been through a lot." He patted Betty on the shoulder. "You did the right thing, Betty."

"Thanks."

"Is she here now?" Campbell asked.

"She is."

Hesitating, Dr. Campbell took a deep breath and let it out. He knocked twice on the door to Kari's room, opened it, and walked in. He didn't see Nichole but did notice that the bathroom door was shut. "Nichole, are you in there?"

"Go away," she yelled.

"Are you okay?"

He waited for a moment and, then, heard her retching. "Nichole, are you sick?"

"I said go away. I'm fine."

Pausing for only a second, he grabbed hold of the doorknob and swung open the door. "Can I do something to . . ." He stared at Nichole, who was standing in front of a mirror fixing her hair. "What the hell is going on, Nichole."

She jumped at the sound of his voice and turned towards him. "Get out of here. I don't want to talk to you."

"You're in here pretending that you're vomiting," he stated. "What do you think you're doing?"

"It's none of your damn business. Now leave me alone."

"Why are you pretending to be sick? You need to tell me," he demanded.

"I just felt sick, that's all. I wasn't pretending."

"Yes, you were, Nichole. What is going on with you?"

Nichole turned and stared at her reflection in the mirror, not answering him. "Do you think I'm still pretty?"

"Are you pregnant, Nichole?" Ben asked her.

Nichole smiled. "Of course, I'm pregnant, Ben. And, you're the father. I thought you would have figured it out before now. You know, you being a doctor and all. Isn't it wonderful?"

Ben backed out of the bathroom, turned, and walked over to the small couch. He sat down, shaking his head. "It can't be mine" he mumbled. "I've had a vasectomy. If you're pregnant, Nichole, I'm certainly not the father."

"Of course, you are, silly man. Do the math. We had sex right around Labor Day. I'm three months pregnant."

"No way," Ben said. "You're not going to pin this on me. I don't know who the father is, but it sure as hell isn't me. I'm not taking the hit for this, Nichole."

Nichole walked over to the side of Kari's bed and picked up a book off of the nightstand. "Move over," she ordered. "I need to sit down." As he started to move to the end of the couch, Nichole rushed towards him, raising the book.

"What are you . . ."

Before Ben could finish his question, Nichole swung the book and slammed it into the side of Ben's face.

Although stunned by what had just happened, Ben was still able to raise his hand and reach for her wrist, hoping to get her under control. Laughing now, Nichole stepped out of his way. She raised the book and hit him again with all the force she could muster up.

“Stop it!” Ben yelled, putting his hands over his face.

As Nichole started to swing the book the third time, she was grabbed from behind.

“That’s enough,” Betty shouted, holding Nichole’s arms behind her back.

“Let me go,” Nichole screamed, trying to break loose.

“Settle down, Nichole. Stop fighting me.”

“Let go of me,” Nichole cried out again, frantically trying to break free of Betty’s grip.

Betty looked over at Ben and shook her head. “Are you okay? You’re bleeding pretty bad.”

“I’m gonna fucking kill her,” he yelled. “I think she broke my nose. Get me a towel, will you” he asked.”

Betty hesitated. “I can’t let go of her. Hold on a minute.” She walked over to Kari’s bed, pushing Nichole in front of her. She reached over and hit the call button.

Within seconds, Marg ran into the room. She glanced around, saw Dr. Campbell bleeding, and Nichole being restrained by Betty. She shook her head. “It looks like you could use some help in here. What in blazes happened?”

“Nichole whacked Dr. Campbell with a book. Come here and hold onto her for me. I need to help the doctor.”

As Marg took hold of Nichole, Betty ran into the bathroom, grabbed a towel, and handed it to the doctor.

Suddenly, Nichole went limp and started to fall to the floor.

"I can't hold her," Marg exclaimed.

"Let the bitch fall," Dr. Campbell yelled, as he put his head back in an attempt to stop the bleeding. "And, get security up here, Marg."

"What about her?" Marg asked as she looked at Nichole.

"Just go," Betty told her. "I've got her if she tries anything."

"Right," Marg called out, as she hurried out of the room.

"Let me help you with that," Betty said, as she took the towel from Dr. Campbell and held it against his nose. "What the hell happened?" Betty asked.

"She went nuts," Campbell told her, angrily. "God, my nose really hurts," he whined. He stared at Nichole, who was still lying on the floor. "I'm gonna kill her. I swear to God, she's dead meat."

"Calm down, Doctor. You don't mean that."

Dr. Campbell took a deep breath. "I'm sorry. It's just that I'm so damn mad." He closed his eyes and took a deep breath. "Please, forget I said that. I didn't mean it."

"I know," Betty said. "It's forgotten." She stood up. "Marg is back. She can watch Nichole. Now, how about you and I go get that nose fixed up?"

Twenty-four

Nichole looked around the room, trying to figure out where she was. It was obvious that she was on a couch in someone's office, but she had no idea who it belonged to. She started to raise her arm to check her watch and realized that her arms were restrained behind her back. "What the hell?" she muttered, and started to yell for help.

As the door started to open, she tried to sit up. "Over here," she cried out. "Help me."

"Calm down, Mrs. Armstrong."

She watched as Ben, along with two men she didn't recognize, walked into the office. "Ben? What's going on?"

"In a moment, Nichole," he abruptly replied.

Nichole watched as the men sat down. Ben looked over at Nichole.

"My, God," Nichole exclaimed as she looked at Ben's bandaged nose. "What happened to you?"

"You don't remember?" Ben asked her.

"Remember what? And, why am I in handcuffs?"

"It's for your own safety, Nichole."

"Well, take them off."

"Nichole, this is Mr. Duffy, who is head of security for the hospital," he declared, motioning to an extremely tall man. "And, this man is Dr. Hoyt, who is a psychiatrist. I discussed what happened a few hours ago in Kari's room with him. He has some concerns about your mental health, as do I."

Nichole looked shocked. "I don't understand, Ben. What would you two possibly have to discuss? There's nothing wrong with my mental health, as you put it. And, will someone please take off these damn cuffs?"

Ben looked over at Duffy. "What do you think?"

"I think we're safe, Dr. Campbell," he said smiling. He stood and walked over to Nichole. "You promise not to break any more noses if I uncuff you?"

"What are you talking about?" Nichole asked, looking confused. "And, what did you mean, Ben, when you said a couple of hours ago? How long have I been here?"

"As I said, a couple of hours," Ben replied. "We sedated you after we couldn't get you to calm down."

"You sedated me? I don't remember that," Nichole said quietly.

"Exactly what is the last thing you remember before you came to?" Dr. Hoyt asked her.

She sat up straight as Duffy took the cuffs off. As she stretched out her arms, she smiled. "That feels better." She took a deep breath and let it out. "Why?"

"Do you remember hitting Dr. Campbell and breaking his nose?"

Nichole laughed. "You're joking, right? Are you saying that I did that?"

"Yes, that's exactly what I'm saying," Dr. Hoyt replied.

Nichole shook her head back and forth. "No, no, no. That can't be right. I would never do anything to hurt Ben. He's the father of . . ."

"Nichole," Dr. Hoyt interrupted, "you are not pregnant. I've talked to Dr. Hazelton."

"But I haven't had my period in months and I've had morning . . ."

"You're not pregnant, Nichole!" Hoyt interrupted. "You've started menopause. I believe Dr. Hazelton explained all of this to you when you last saw her."

Nichole glared at him. "Well, she's wrong. I'm too young to be going through menopause. Anyway, I'm not seeing her anymore. I'm going to find a new doctor."

"Have you taken any of the medication that Dr. Hazelton prescribed for your mood swings and anxiety?" Hoyt asked.

"Of course not. I'm not taking that crap. I just told you that I'm not going through menopause."

"Nichole, you attacked Dr. Campbell, broke his nose, and you don't remember doing it. You have a hormonal imbalance and it's probably the worst I've ever seen in a patient. You need help."

"I am not your patient, Dr. Hoyt," Nichole declared. "And, I refuse to put that crap into my body."

"Ben, would you like to tell Nichole her options here?" Hoyt asked.

"Nichole, we're all concerned about you. With everything that you've been through, the last thing you needed was for menopause to hit you like a ton of bricks. But it has happened and you are experiencing the ultimate side effects and it's driving you over the edge."

"Am not," Nichole said softly.

"Yes, you are," Ben replied. "So, taking into consideration your problems, I'm going to give you a few options here. So, listen carefully. Okay?"

Nichole sighed. "Okay."

"The first one is having you arrested for assaulting me. If you're found guilty – and I'll make damn sure you are – you'll probably do jail time."

Nichole stared at him, obviously shocked. "You'd do that to me? I can't. . ."

"Quiet! Just listen. Number two. Mr. Duffy will post your picture at every entrance and you will no longer be allowed in this hospital . . ."

"No!" Nichole shouted. "You can't do that."

"I can and I will," Ben told her. "Three, Dr. Hoyt will have you admitted to Clariton and have you placed under observation for ninety days."

"I'm not nuts," Nichole yelled.

"Clariton is a mental health facility, Nichole. And, right now, if I had my choice, that's where I'd send you."

Nichole glared at him. "You hate me, don't you?"

"You damn right I hate you. You broke my fucking nose. A person with all their faculties doesn't act that way, Nichole. You have a problem and it's time you understand that."

"I think you should be thankful for what Dr. Campbell is doing for you. If it was anyone else, Nichole, they would be sitting behind bars right now," Dr. Hoyt interjected. "Ben, you want to finish up?"

"Thank you, Doctor. Fourth, Nichole, you will agree to have weekly hormone shots to get yourself under control. These injections will be administered by Dr. Hazelton and she will monitor your condition and will give us an update after every shot. If you miss even one appointment, you will no longer be allowed in this hospital to see Kari."

"You can't make me," Nichole mumbled.

Dr. Campbell sat back in his chair and stared at her. "To reiterate - one is jail, two is not being allowed in the hospital and never seeing Kari again, three is Clariton, and four is getting hormone shots."

Nichole looked down, not saying anything.

"Well?" Dr. Hoyt finally said.

"I'm thinking," she told him.

Duffy looked over at Ben, shaking his head. "I don't fucking believe this woman."

"Nichole?" Ben asked.

"Well, obviously, it's number four. I'm not crazy, you know."

"One more thing, Nichole," Ben said.

"What now?" she asked, giving him a disgusted look.

"I'm turning Kari over to my partner, Dr. Belle Dunbar. I will no longer have any contact with you or Kari."

"No!" Nichole yelled. "You're Kari's doctor. I can't agree to someone else."

"And, you are not to approach me if you see me in the hospital. Is that clear?"

"But, Ben, there's got to be another way for you to still be Kari's doctor. Please," she pleaded, starting to cry.

Ben shook his head no. "I don't trust you, Nichole. Sorry, but no."

"I'll do anything you want. Please," she begged, looking at him through her tears.

Totally ignoring her, Ben stood up and walked to the door. He turned and looked back at the two men. "Dr. Hoyt, thank you for your guidance in this matter. Mr.

Duffy, please make sure that Nichole makes it to her car safely. Good day, gentlemen."

Nichole stared as he walked away.

"Mrs. Armstrong?"

"What?"

"You have an appointment with Dr. Hazelton at eight a.m. tomorrow morning. Make sure you are on time," Dr. Hoyt stated. "I will be checking with her. If you fail to keep this or any of the appointments, you will be barred from the hospital. You do understand that, don't you?"

Nichole wiped her eyes with the back of her hand and glared at him.

"This is for your own good, you know. We only have your best interests in mind."

"Fine," Nichole said. "I'll keep this appointment. But I'm also going to have a long talk with my attorney about what has happened here today. You're forcing me to take medication that I don't want to take. You people have held me against my will and have threatened to keep me away from my daughter. You have no right."

"You broke Dr. Campbell's nose and I don't recall anyone giving you the right to do that. You better think long and hard about the consequences before you start talking lawyer, Nichole," Hoyt declared.

Twenty-five

Christmas Day

"Do you realize that this is the second Christmas you've spent here, Kari?" Nichole mentioned. She reached for Kari's hand and stroked it. "I only did a little decorating this year, but I did buy you a few presents. Time has gone so fast, hasn't it? You'd be a sophomore in college now if you hadn't been in that accident."

She reached for a tissue and blew her nose. "I sure hope I'm not getting a cold. My nose has been running all day."

Nichole stood and walked over to her purse. She opened it and removed a book. "I brought A Christmas Carol to read to you today. It used to be one of your favorites. Keith's, too. Remember, when you two were little, we'd light the Christmas tree and you two would climb up on my lap and snuggle close while I read this book to you?"

Nichole sat back down by Kari and opened the book. "Okay. Ready?" She flipped through the first few pages, found the page she wanted, and started to read. '*Stave 1, Marley's Ghost. Marley was dead to begin with. There is no doubt whatever about that. The register of his burial was signed by the clergyman, the clerk, the undertaker, and the chief mourner. Scrooge signed it; and. . ."*

"Do you mind if I listen, too?"

"Be my guest," Nichole replied, as she glanced over at the door to see who was speaking. Totally shocked, she let the book drop to the floor. "Keith?" she whispered. "Oh my God, Keith, is that you?"

"Hi, Mom. Merry Christmas."

As the tears started rolling down her cheeks, Nichole jumped up and ran to her son. She threw her arms around him and hugged him as hard as she could. "It's you. It's really you," she cried, as she started showering kisses all over his face. She stepped back and looked at him from the top of his head to his feet. "You've grown," she declared, laughing.

"A full three inches," Keith replied proudly.

Nichole pulled him close and hugged him again. "You're beautiful. My beautiful boy. Oh, I've missed you so much."

"I've missed you, too, Mom."

"I need to sit," Nichole told him, as she walked over to the couch. "Here, sit beside me," she said, as she patted the cushion.

Keith sat down beside her and smiled as she took his hand. "How is Kari doing?" he asked. He looked at his sister. "She looks like she's sleeping, doesn't she? It breaks my heart to see her like this."

"She's about the same as she was the last time you saw her. A little thinner, maybe. I pray every day that she either wakes up or that God takes her." Nichole squeezed his hand. "We have so much to talk about, Keith. Oh, my God, I can't believe you're really here." She looked into his eyes. "You're staying, aren't you? Please tell me you're staying."

"If it's okay with you," Keith told her. "But you should know that there's a lot of stuff that needs to be straightened out."

"Of course, it's okay. You can stay forever and ever. And, we're not going to worry about all that other stuff today. Today is Christmas and a day for celebrating. My boy has come home."

"Is there any food in that home? 'Cause to tell you the truth, Mom, I'm starving."

Nichole smiled. "Same old Keith. Always hungry."

"I guess," he said.

"Let's say goodbye to Kari and, then, go home," Nichole said. "You can open your presents, although I'm not sure if they are going to fit."

"You bought me presents?" Keith asked, surprised.

"Of course, it's Christmas, isn't it?"

Nichole went to the side of Kari's bed, bent down, and kissed her goodbye. "I'm leaving now, Kari. But I just got the best present. Keith is here. He misses you so much. Anyway, we're going home and I'm going to fix your brother something to eat. Merry Christmas, darling."

"Do you still think she can hear you?" Keith asked.

"I can only hope," Nichole replied, as she grabbed her coat. "Let's go."

Keith sat back in the chair and burped. "Sorry. S'cuse me," he said.

"You're excused. Good pizza, isn't it?"

"The best." He looked at the last piece of pizza on the table.

"Take it," Nichole said.

"You sure?"

"I'm sure," Nichole told him, laughing. "I couldn't eat another bite."

"Do you still make Christmas cookies?" Keith asked her.

Nichole shook her head no. “No reason to, Keith. It’s just been me here and, to tell you the truth, the holidays haven’t meant much to me the past couple of years.”

“How’s dad doing? Do you ever talk to him?”

“Occasionally. I try to let the attorneys handle whatever needs to be taken care of. Our divorce is final, of course. Fortunately, with a little help from your grandparents, I managed to buy him out and keep the house. The biggest problem we have now is that he still wants to take Kari off life support.”

Keith shook his head. “I can’t believe you guys are still fighting about that.”

“How do you feel about that, Keith? Your father and I never asked you how you felt about that and we were wrong. Do you think I’m still making a mistake, hoping that she may wake up one day?”

“You know what, Mom? Que Sera, Sera. It’s not up to you or dad.” Keith leaned back and stretched. “I’m tired. Would you mind if I took a shower and hopped into bed?”

“I guess not,” Nichole said, looking disappointed.

“I really am tired, Mom.”

“Of course, you are. It’s just that I’ve got a million questions to ask you, but I guess they can wait until tomorrow.”

“Good,” Keith said as he stood up.

“You go take your shower. I’m going to go to the store and buy some groceries.”

“Seriously? It’s nine o’clock on Christmas Eve. What’s even open?”

“Walmart. They never close.”

"Even Christmas Eve?"

"And, Christmas Day."

"That is just wrong," Keith declared.

"Do you still eat cereal for breakfast?"

Keith grinned. "I eat anything that's available, but cereal is fine. But, please, none that's loaded with sugar. Okay?"

"Got it." Nichole walked over to him and hugged him. "I can't believe you're here. It looks like prayers do work. I love you, Keith."

"Love you, too, Mom," Keith replied, as he wiggled out of her grasp. "I smell and it's time for a shower. See you in the morning."

"Sleep tight, my love."

Twenty-six

"And, that's about it," Nichole declared, as she finished off her coffee and set the cup down.

Keith looked at her and shook his head. "Wow! You've really had a rough time, haven't you? I had no idea that menopause could drive a woman crazy."

Nichole laughed. "To tell you the truth, neither did I. I still can't believe that I broke Dr. Campbell's nose, but it was probably a good thing."

"A good thing?" Keith asked, surprised at her comment.

"It forced me to get the medication that I needed. I've had four shots now and I feel like a different person. I didn't know how bad I had gotten. I've apologized to everyone and Dr. Campbell says he forgives me, but I don't think he does. His nose healed kind of crooked and he hates it. Word on the street is that he's going to have it reset. I never realized he was so vain."

"If I remember right, he was a pretty good-looking guy, wasn't he?" Keith asked.

"I guess. Whatever. At least I don't have to worry about not being allowed in the hospital to see Kari."

"Well, I'm glad you're feeling better," Keith told her. "Now, how about giving Sheriff Katts a call and let him know I'm here."

"I have a better idea. How about we get through the holidays and wait until after New Year's? I'd like to spend more time with you before you talk to him. And, you haven't even seen your dad yet."

Keith smiled. "I want to get this over with, Mom. I have no idea what is going to happen. If Sheriff Katts doesn't believe me, I could wind up behind bars."

"And, that is why you should wait," Nichole commented.

"Nice try. No, I want to get this over with. Do you want to call him or should I?"

Nichole sighed, resigned to the fact that she wasn't going to be able to change Keith's mind. "All right. I'll call him, but I wish you would wait."

Nichole stood in the entry and waited. The Sheriff's car had just pulled into her driveway and she was waiting for him to come to the door. Keith was sitting in the living room watching TV. How can he be so relaxed, Nichole wondered, as she glanced over at her son.

She threw open the door before Carson had a chance to ring the bell. "Hi, Carson. Come on in."

Carson looked her up and down and grinned. "You are looking real fine this morning, Nichole."

"Thank you. So are you."

"So, what can I do for you? You didn't say much when you called." He said, grinning. "I was kind of hoping you might have had second thoughts about . . ."

"Keith's here," Nichole interrupted before he could finish his sentence.

"You're kidding," he said, looking surprised.

"He wants to talk to you."

"And, I sure as hell want to talk to him. Where is he?"

"In the living room."

As Nichole and Carson walked into the living room, Keith grabbed the remote, turned off the TV, and stood up. "Sheriff Katts, it's nice to see you."

"It's good to see you, too, Keith. It's been a while."

"It has," Keith responded.

"Coffee?" Nichole asked.

"Oh, yeah. And, keep it coming. I have a feeling I'm gonna be here for a while."

Carson settled himself into an overstuffed chair. He took a pad and pen out of his shirt pocket, looked at Keith, and smiled. "Well, Keith, do you want to tell me what you've been up to for the past year?"

Keith glanced over at his mother, a worried look on his face. "Where should I start?"

Nichole smiled. "Go ahead, Keith. Just tell him what you told me."

Keith scratched his forehead, thinking about what to say. "Okay, first of all, I did not kill Hunter Davis. Neither did Jason. We did beat him up, though." He hesitated.

"Go on," Carson said.

"When I left here a year ago, I was really pissed. For six months, I listened to my mom and dad fight night after night about Kari. Pull the plug! Don't pull the plug! I had had it and I stormed out. I was going to come back. I didn't intend to stay away, but I ran into Jason."

"Jason Krueger was here? In town?"

"Yeah. He comes here a lot. Anyway, we got to talking and he said I should come and stay with him and his mom for a while. You, know, just until things settled down. So, I went to Milwaukee."

"You drove your car there?" Carson asked.

"Yeah. I followed him. He had his own car."

"You stayed with him from the night you left here until now?"

"Pretty much. I took a few little trips checking out a few towns in Wisconsin. I thought about staying in Madison for a while. I figured I could get lost in the crowd of all those college kids. You know, get a job somewhere and settle in."

"How long were you there?"

"A couple of days. I didn't like it, so I went back to Jason's. We didn't do much. Jason had already dropped out of school, so we just hung around."

"Doesn't Jason have a job?" Carson asked.

"Nah. His mom gives him money when he needs it, but he mostly gets his money by selling a little weed."

"Just weed?"

"A few pills now and then, but mostly weed. And, that's where the problem started."

"Problem?"

"Well, I kinda started selling it, too. It was a way to make a little money. I . . ." Keith gave his mom a questioning look.

"Tell him, Keith," Nichole said.

"I started using. I'd never smoked pot or taken any pills before and – well, I liked it. Jason and I partied almost every night. The truth is, I was high most of the time."

"So, basically what you're telling me is that you have been with Jason and his mom almost the entire year you've been gone. And, you've not only been using drugs but you've been selling them. Is that right?"

"Pretty much."

"So, what happened with Hunter Douglas?"

"Mom, can I get a Coke or something to drink?"

"I'll get it. Carson, can I get you more coffee while I'm up?"

Carson handed her his cup. "Thanks." He looked over at Keith. "Tell me what happened the night that Hunter was killed. And, don't leave anything out."

Keith pursed his lips and let out a big sigh. "First of all, as I said, we didn't kill him. When we last saw him, he was alive. And, he was the one who actually started the fight."

Carson's head jerked up and he stared at Keith. "Are you telling me that Douglas started a fight with you two guys? He may be big, but he'd have to be nuts to try to take you both on."

"I know. And, don't you think he had to be a little nuts when he ran Logan's car off the road, trying to kill my sister? Besides, he started the fight with me. I don't think he realized that Jason was with me."

"How can you be sure it was him that caused the accident?"

"He told us. He was pissed because Kari had dumped him and was dating Logan."

"Let's back up a little. Where did you and Jason run into Hunter?"

"One of Jason's friends had a party we went to and Hunter was there. The minute he saw me, he went ballistic. We took it outside and I kicked the shit out of him. Hunter and I both had bloody noses, plus he had quite a few cuts and bruises."

"Did you hit him with any kind of a weapon?"

Keith looked surprised. "No. Of course not. It was a fistfight, plain and simple."

"Was Hunter ever in your car?"

Again, looking surprised, Keith shook his head no. "No. As far as I know, never. Why?"

"I'm having some problem believing you Keith. You should know that we found Hunter's blood in the back seat and the trunk of your car. Do you want to explain how it got there?"

Keith thought for a moment. "As I said, we both had bloody noses. Plus, Hunter had some cuts. He bled a lot and a lot of his blood got on my shirt. It must have been from his blood getting on my shirt."

Carson looked up at him. "How did his blood get in the trunk of your car, then?"

"I threw my bloody shirt in the trunk. It must have gotten on the carpet." Keith shrugged. "That's the only way it could have gotten there because Hunter was never in my car."

Carson glanced over at Nichole. "It's possible that the blood was transferred to the trunk from the shirt, but I'm finding it hard to believe this, Nichole."

"Well, that's what happened," Keith told him. "We left the party and we didn't see Hunter again."

"Where was this party you say you went to?"

"It was at a big house out on County Hwy K."

"Who owns the house?"

"I'm not really sure what their name is. Jason's friend's name is Jake." He thought for a moment. "Jake Williams. That's it. Jake Williams."

Carson glanced at his watch, checking the time. "I have a lot more questions for you, Keith. Perhaps, we should continue this down at the station."

"No!" Nichole cried out. "Please, Carson, don't take him down there."

"I don't have much choice, Nichole. He admits he was with Hunter before he was killed. I have to take him in."

"No, you don't. Besides, what proof do you have that Keith had anything to do with Hunter's murder? None! So, do me a favor and let him stay here with me for now. I promise he'll be here anytime you need to talk to him." She waited for him to answer her. "Please, Carson."

"It's almost eleven. I've got an appointment I need to get to." He looked at Nichole and smiled. "He stays here. Understand?"

"Yes. Thank you."

"Keith, I want you to write down the names of everyone that was at that party."

"I didn't know any of them until that night."

"Well, try to remember. They just might be your alibi, if they can verify that Hunter was alive when you and Jason left that party. Also, you are not to leave this house. Consider yourself under house arrest, until I say different."

"Yes, sir. Thank you, Sheriff Katts."

"I'll be back this afternoon, Nichole. I'm no way near finished with Keith. We still have a lot to talk about."

"I'm off to see Kari," Nichole told Keith, a few minutes after Carson left. "I'd ask you to come along, but you can't leave the house."

“I know. I’d like to see dad, though. Is it all right if I call him and ask him to come over?”

Nichole hesitated a moment. “I don’t want him here, Keith.”

“Come on, Mom. What’s he gonna do? How about I make sure he’s gone before you get back?”

“I don’t know” She hesitated a few seconds. “I guess it’s okay. I’ll be back around two or a little after. Just make sure he’s gone before that, okay?”

“Absolutely. Thanks, Mom.”

“See you later,” Nichole called out as she opened the door. “Love you.”

Twenty-seven

"Are you kidding me?" Sheriff Katts mumbled as he walked into the police station. Deputy Truhouse was leaning back in his chair, eyes closed, feet up on his desk, and he was snoring. "Truhouse," Katts yelled. "Wake the hell up."

Truhouse opened one eye and looked at Katts. "I'm awake. I was thinking."

"Do you always snore while you think?" Katts asked him.

Truhouse yawned. "Sorry. I did a double shift yesterday and I'm beat. Did you need something?"

"Yeah. First off, I need for you to wake up. Then, I want you to check on a kid for me. His name is Jake Williams. He lives out on County Hwy K in one of those expensive big houses."

"What am I looking for?" Truhouse asked.

"See if he has any priors and try to find out what his connection is to Jason Krueger. According to Keith Armstrong, he and Jason were at a party there the night Hunter Douglas was killed."

"You talked to Keith Armstrong? Where'd you find him?"

"He showed up at the hospital yesterday. He's back at home."

Truhouse stood up and grabbed his hat. "Aren't you going to bring him in?"

"Not yet. I want to talk to him some more and I figure he will be more comfortable in his own house. If you talk to Williams, try to get the names of everyone at that party."

"You think Williams had something to do with Douglas' murder?"

"If he didn't, he may know who did." Katts watched as Truhouse walked to the door. "Oh, and Mikey?"

Truhouse turned and looked at him. "Yeah?"

"If he gives you any trouble, bring him in."

"Will do," Truhouse told him.

"And, take a uniform with you," Katts added.

"So, you do figure there's gonna be a problem."

Katts shrugged. "You never know. Better to be on the safe side."

"Oh, Kari, I wish you'd been there. It's so wonderful having Keith back home. Of course, we still don't know if Sheriff Katts is going to press any charges. Keith says he was with that Krueger boy most of the time he was gone and it sounds like he got into some bad stuff. He seems fine now, though, so, hopefully, he's put all that behind him." Nichole walked over to Kari's bed. "Your pillow seems a little bunched up." She reached over and adjusted Kari's pillow. "There, is that better?"

"How are you doing today, Nichole?"

Nichole turned and smiled. "I'm fine, Betty. How about you?"

"I'm good."

"Are you feeling okay?" Betty asked her, smiling.

Nichole grinned. "Nothing to worry about, Betty. I'm doing okay."

"I hear you've kept all your appointments with Dr. Mabel. I'm glad."

"Me, too. And, again, I apologize for anything I said or did that was out of line. I wasn't myself for a while."

"I know and don't you worry about it."

Nichole watched as Betty checked out Kari. "Betty?" Nichole said, after a few moments.

Betty looked over at her. "Yes?"

"Have you noticed any more unusual movements on Kari's monitor? Has it happened again?"

Betty looked away, not saying anything.

"You have, haven't you?" Nichole exclaimed.

Betty looked around the room. "I shouldn't say anything, but there's been a couple of times that something showed up, but we still don't know what's causing it. And, one time . . ." Betty glanced over at the door to be sure no one was listening. "One time," she continued, whispering now, "when I was in here, I saw her leg move. Well, it was more of a jerk, than a move, but it happened. You were right, Nichole when you said you saw her move."

"Thank you, Betty. Sometimes, when I have almost convinced myself to let her go, I hear something like this, or I see her move and I just can't do it. I just can't give up hope."

"I don't blame you. I don't know if I could do what you've done. You're a strong woman, Nichole. Most people would have given up a long time ago. Kari is a lucky girl to have a mom like you."

"Thank you, Betty."

"You want to hear something funny?"

Nichole smiled. "I could use a laugh. What?"

"Well, I can tell you this, now that you're all better. For a while, I thought that you and Dr. Campbell had a thing going on. He was always so concerned about you and, sometimes, the way you looked at him . . . Well, I just thought you two had connected."

Nichole laughed. "Really?"

"The best part, though, is when you thought you were pregnant. I actually thought you were, too, and I thought that Dr. Campbell was the father. Isn't that just the silliest thing?"

"Oh, Betty," Nichole said, trying not to react to her comments, "you do have quite the imagination, don't you?"

"Well, enough foolishness for today. I've got to get busy." Betty glanced over at Nichole, as she started to leave the room. She stopped and grinned.

"What?" Nichole inquired.

"Why, Nichole, you're blushing. Maybe, I wasn't so far off, after all."

"Don't be silly. It's probably just a hot flash," she told her, laughing.

Twenty-eight

Sheriff Katts had just pulled into his driveway when he heard his phone ding, indicating that he had a text. He pulled out his phone and saw that the message was from Deputy Truhouse. *Milwaukee police just picked up Jason Krueger. Are holding him. Call Sheriff Potts.*

"Good show," he exclaimed, as he texted Truhouse back. *At my house. Send me phone number.* He opened his car door, got out, and looked up at the sky. Looks like snow, he thought.

Nichole picked up her phone and saw that it was Sheriff Katts calling. "Hi, Carson. What's up?"

"Something came up, Nichole. I'm not going to be able to come back over to talk to Keith today."

"I see. Well, that's fine."

"I'd like to see Keith tomorrow. How about I give you a call in the morning and let you know what time."

Nichole thought for a moment. "That should be okay," she finally said. "Do you know how long it will take?"

"Until I'm done, Nichole. One never knows how these things will go."

"I guess. Okay, Carson, I'll see you tomorrow."

"How did it go with Jake Williams?" Katts asked Truhouse when he got back to the station.

"It went fine. He seems like a nice enough kid. He admits to having a party and that there was a fight. He said that Hunter went ballistic when he saw Keith. He also said that after Hunter had the crap beat out of him, Keith and Jason left the party. Said it was around eleven or so. He wasn't sure of the exact time. I'm going back out there later today."

"What for?"

"The party was a long time ago and he was kinda foggy about who was there. He's putting a list together for me. I told him I'd pick it up later today."

"Bull. You call him and tell him to drop it off here," Katts told him.

"If you don't mind, Sheriff, I'd like to drive out and get it."

Katts stared at him for a few seconds. "Good-looking sister?" he asked, grinning.

"What?" Truhouse said, acting insulted. "What do you think I am? A cradle robber."

"Then, it's got to be the mother," Katts declared.

"She's a real knockout, Sheriff," Truhouse said, blushing.

At eight-thirty the next morning, Katts set his coffee cup on the kitchen table. He pulled a pad and a pen out of his pocket and sat down. He glanced over at Jason Krueger and looked away. He took a sip of his coffee. "Hmm. That tastes good. I don't know how he does it, but Deputy Truhouse makes the best coffee I've ever tasted."

Jason looked at him. "That's nice."

"We had a lot of snow last night."

Jason stared at him, wondering what the hell he was talking about.

“How was your ride here from Milwaukee? Did everything go okay?”

“I’m here, aren’t I?”

“You certainly are, and I can’t tell you how happy I am to see you.” Katts took another sip of his coffee. “So, where have you been for the past two months, Jason?”

“Around.”

“You know you’re in some serious trouble, don’t you? It looks like you and your pal, Keith, are gonna go away for a long, long time.”

“So, I skipped bail. That’s no big deal,” he said arrogantly.

“Ah, but it is, Jason.”

“Besides, what does Keith have to do with it? He didn’t skip bail.”

“No, he didn’t. However, skipping bail isn’t the main reason you’re here.”

“Then, what is?”

“Why, murder, of course. You’re going down for the murder of Hunter Douglas. We know you and your friend, Keith Armstrong, killed that kid.”

Jason stared at him for a moment, then, laughed. “No way, man. We didn’t kill him and you know it.”

“Well, according to Keith you did. He’s already told us all about how you two beat Douglas up and, then, stabbed him. You can tell me your side of the story if you want, but I don’t need it. I’ve got everything I need to put you away for a long time.” Katts closed his notebook and stood up. “Think about it for a few minutes, Jason.”

“You’re lying. Keith never said that,” Jason yelled, as he watched Katts walk out of the room.

Katts turned around and stared at him. "Am I? I know you went to a party at Jake Williams' house. I know that while you were there, you and Keith got into a fight with Douglas. I know you left the party and waited down the road until Douglas left the party. I know that you followed him, ran him off the road, and stabbed him to death."

Jason shook his head. "No!" he yelled. "That's all messed up, man."

"Is it? Think about it, Jason," he said, smirking. He walked out and closed the door.

"How much longer are you gonna make that kid sit in there?" Deputy Truhouse asked Katts.

"A little longer," Katts replied.

"He's been alone in there for over an hour now."

"I know. I want to give him plenty of time to think about what I said."

"You don't think he'll see through all those lies?"

"Nah, he's too dumb. Why don't you go ask him if he needs anything?"

"Like what?" Truhouse inquired.

"Like something to drink. Perhaps he'd like another can of soda."

Truhouse grinned and went over to the room where Krueger was being held. He opened the door and stuck his head into the room. "You need anything?" he asked Jason.

Jason picked his head up off the small table and looked up at Truhouse. "I need to pee," he told him.

"I'll check with the boss," Truhouse said. "Do you want anything to drink? Are you hungry?"

Jason looked at him like he was crazy. "No, you idiot. I don't want anything to drink. Didn't you just hear me tell you I have to pee?"

"Yeah, I heard you," Truhouse stated as he started to shut the door.

"Wait! Let me out of here," Jason yelled. "I have to pee!"

Truhouse grinned. "Hell, man, you've got an empty can right there. Go for it," he said, pointing to the empty soda can. Laughing, he shut the door.

An hour later, Katts looked up from his desk. "Well, I guess I should go see if Jason has anything to tell me."

"Good luck with that," Truhouse said. "Do you think he used the soda can?"

"I sure as hell hope not," Katts replied laughing.

"How are you doing, Jason?" Katts asked as he entered the room.

Jason glared at him. "You people are really mean," he whined.

"What do you mean by that?" Katts inquired, looking surprised.

"I'm telling my lawyer that you wouldn't let me pee."

"No, no, no, Jason. You can go to the bathroom if you have to. Besides, you don't have a lawyer."

"I can?" he replied, looking confused.

"Of course, you can. Just as soon as you tell me if it was you or if it was Keith who killed Hunter Douglas. Keith says it was you that stabbed him. Is he telling the truth?" Katts sat down across the table and stared at Jason.

"Keith's a fucking liar," Jason said, looking away.

Katts didn't respond.

"All right!" Jason yelled after a few moments. "How about I tell you the truth about everything? But, first, you have to let me go to the john. I'm gonna explode here, man. I don't think I can hold it any longer," Jason said, squirming in his chair.

"I don't know," Katts said, dragging the words out. He looked up at the ceiling, pretending to think about it. "It's a deal. But you better not hold anything back," he finally said.

"Fine. Just uncuff me," Jason cried out. "Hurry up, man."

Katts reached over and removed Jason's cuffs. "Second door to your right," he said, grinning, as Jason made a mad dash for the door.

Ninety minutes later, Katts walked out of the interview room.

Deputy Truhouse looked up from his desk. "Finished?" he asked.

"For now."

"Did he kill the Douglas kid?

"He says he didn't have anything to do with the murder."

"He won't fess up, huh?" Truhouse inquired.

"Nope. But he told me who did it."

Truhouse stared at him. "You're kidding. Was it Keith Armstrong?"

"He says it was, but he wasn't there when Douglas was killed, so it's just his word."

"Do you think Keith did it?"

Katts shook his head. “I can’t see him killing anyone. I’ve known this kid for years. I was his coach. I’ll be shocked if I find out it really was him. Anyway, take him over to holding for the night, Mikey.”

“Can I go home, then? I’ve been going for almost eighteen hours without any sleep.”

Katts grinned. “I think you’re the only person I know who snores while he’s awake, Mikey.”

“I was just resting my eyes,” Truhouse declared.

“Yeah, right,” Katts replied.

Twenty-nine

"Jason Krueger has informed me that you killed Hunter Douglas."

"What? Wait a minute. When did you talk to Jason?" Keith asked, surprised.

"We have him in custody."

"If he told you that, then, he's a fu . . . He glanced over at his mother. "He's a rotten liar," he told Carson.

"I had a long talk with him yesterday and he told me everything." He opened his pad of paper and started going over his notes. "He said that you beat Douglas up at the party."

"I already told you that. And, Jason helped. He's not innocent here."

"Right," Carson said, still looking at his notes. "Wait a minute, here. You said that you beat up Hunter. Are you now telling me that Jason was part of that fight?"

"I kinda remember him kicking Hunter a few times after . . ." He looked away. "After Hunter was down, Jason gave him a few kicks to the ribs."

"I see. He also told us that after you left the party, you parked down the road and waited for Hunter to leave. You followed him after he left the party, ran him off the road, and stabbed him to death."

Keith shook his head no. "Mom?" he cried out. "I didn't do that. You've got to believe me. I didn't kill him. I would never hurt anyone."

"Really, Keith?" Carson said. "You just admitted to beating the crap out of Douglas, and you can sit there and say you'd never hurt anybody? What do you expect me to believe?"

"Hunter started that fight. I was only defending myself, Coach," Keith said.

"It's Sheriff, Keith. I'm not your coach today. I'm Sheriff Katts."

"Sorry," Keith replied, looking down at the floor.

"Let's go over it one more time. From the time you and Jason got to the party."

Nichole closed her eyes and sighed. "Must he, Carson? He's already told you everything he knows. Give him a break, will you?"

"I'm already giving him a break, Nichole. If I wasn't, I'd be talking to him down at the station and he'd be spending time in a cell with his old friend, Jason."

"It's okay, Mom," Keith told her. He looked over at Carson. "What do you want to know, Sheriff Katts?"

"Did Jason get invited to that party or did you two crash it?"

"Jason was invited. Jake Williams and Jason have been friends for years, going back to grade school. Even after Williams moved to the country and went to a different school, they kept in touch. Jason has a lot of old friends around here. I'm not sure, but I think a lot of it has to do with drugs."

"So, he was invited to the party at the Williams' house?"

"As far as I know, he was," Keith said.

"Do you know what the connection between Hunter Douglas and Williams was?"

"No. You'd have to ask Jake about that."

Carson paused long enough to make some notes.

"You said that when Hunter saw you at the party, he started a fight. Why would he do that? He must have known he couldn't take the two of you."

"Again, he came after me. Not Jason. I think he was either high or drunk. But it might have been . . ." Keith hesitated.

"Might have been what, Keith?"

"Well, after Kari's accident, I told him to watch his back – that someday when he least expected it, he was going to get his. But I was just mouthing off, Sheriff. I didn't really intend to hurt him."

"Oh, Keith," Nichole said, getting upset, "why would you do that?"

"It was just stupid talk, Mom. Besides, it was right after Kari got hurt. If I was going to do something to Hunter, don't you think I would have done it a long time ago?"

Carson thought for a moment. "And, you and Jason left the party right after the fight. Is that correct?"

"Yeah. I was pretty bloody from being hit in the nose. I just wanted to get out of there."

"I see. And, where did you go after you left the party?"

"I wanted to drive back to Milwaukee, but Jason wasn't ready to leave yet. He dropped me off and said he was gonna go see a friend of his."

"And, his friend's name?" Carson asked.

Keith got a blank look on his face. "His name?"

"Yes, Keith. What was the name of Jason's friend?"

"I don't remember. Mary or Margie. I think it was something like that. I'm not sure."

"So, he was going to see a girl," Carson declared.

"Yeah. I'm pretty sure I know where the house is."

"Okay, that's something. What's the address?"

Again, Keith looked confused. "Address? I don't know. If the girl is who I think she is, I only know where the house is. I don't know the address."

"All right. I'll have you show me. Where did Jason drop you off?"

Keith glanced over at his mom. "I can't tell you. Mom will get upset."

"I'm not going to get upset," Nichole told him. "Tell him where you went, Keith.

"I can't."

"You can and you will, Keith," Carson declared, "or I'll haul your ass down to the station right now."

"I went to my dad's," he mumbled after a few seconds.

"You what?" Nichole yelled. "Do you mean to tell me that your father has known for almost eight months that you were okay and he didn't let me know? All that time, worrying about you and not knowing if you were alive or dead and . . ." Nichole sat back and stared at Keith. "Why him? Why did you go to him and not me?"

"I needed clean clothes and a place to stay. It's not like I chose him over you, Mom."

"Yeah, it kinda is, Keith," Nichole replied.

"Can we get back on track here?" Carson asked. "I don't care whose house he picked. How long did you stay at your dad's?"

"Until the next day. Jason picked me up and we drove back to Milwaukee the next afternoon."

"What time did you get to your dad's house?"

"I think we left the party around ten-thirty or so . . . I guess I got to dad's around eleven-fifteen. I'm not totally sure."

"And, your dad will verify the time?" Carson asked.

"He should," Keith replied.

"So, you got to your dad's house – let's say between eleven and eleven-thirty and you were there the rest of the night? You never went out again? Is that correct?" Carson asked, making notes.

"Right," Keith answered.

"And, your dad was also there all the time?" Carson asked.

Keith hesitated.

"Keith?" Nichole prompted. "Was he there?"

"I think so."

"What do you mean, you think so? Was he or wasn't he?" Carson asked loudly.

"I can't be sure. When I got there, we talked for a while. I told him what had happened and asked him if I could spend the night. He said it was okay and we both decided to get some sleep. I washed up and crawled into bed. I didn't hear a thing until I woke up the next morning. So, I can't be sure because I was sleeping."

Carson sat back and smiled. "That makes sense. I guess that's about it, then. You were with your dad when Hunter was killed. I'll talk to your dad and if he confirms what time you got to his house . . . Well, you're good, as far as I'm concerned."

"Okay," Keith mumbled, looking uncomfortable.

Nichole stared at her son, feeling uneasy. "Keith, what aren't you telling us?"

"Nothing," Keith replied defensively.

Nichole stared at her son. “Keith?”

“I told you everything. Now leave me alone,” he yelled.

“Keith Bradley Armstrong, enough is enough! Out with it.”

Keith gave her a dirty look.

“Now!” she yelled. “And, don’t you give me that look, young man.”

“Keith, your mom is right. If there is something else we should know, it would be in your best interest to tell us now,” Carson said.

Keith glanced at his mother. “I’m sorry I yelled.”

“It’s okay, sweetie,” Nichole said. “And, I’m sorry I yelled at you.”

“It’s nothing. It’s just that, when I got ready to leave dad’s house, I noticed that his car had been moved. It was parked in a different spot than the one it was in when I got to his house.”

Carson sat back in his chair, thinking about what Keith had told him. “Maybe, your dad had gone out before you woke up,” he suggested.

Keith shook his head no.

“Are you sure, Keith?” Nichole asked.

“I was up before him, and he didn’t leave the house while I was still there.”

“Shit!” Carson exclaimed.

“What does this mean, Carson?” Nichole asked. “Surely, you don’t think Blake had anything to do with Hunter’s death.”

Thirty

"Hey, Carson," Blake exclaimed. "Long time no see."

"How are you doing, Blake?"

"I'm doing okay, everything considered. What brings you here?"

"We need to talk."

"We do?" Blake asked. "What about?"

"Your son and Hunter Douglas' murder."

Blake, looking slightly uncomfortable, opened the door. "Well, if we must, we must. Come on in and sit down and tell me what you're talking about."

Carson stepped into the duplex and looked around. "Nice," he observed.

"It's okay. It's not as nice as my old house, but I'm comfortable here. Why don't we go into the kitchen? I'll put on a pot of coffee."

"Only if you want some. I'm coffeed out."

"This way," Blake told him and showed him the way to the kitchen. "Have a seat," he said, motioning to the table and chairs.

Carson sat down and looked around. "How old is this place?"

"They were built in 2010. I was lucky to get one. They don't go on the market that often and when they do, they sell fast." Blake opened up the refrigerator and took out a beer. "Want one?" he asked.

"No, thanks. I'm on duty," Carson said.

"I figured," Blake said. "What's this about?"

"I understand that Keith spent a night here back in May."

You know about that?" Blake asked, looking surprised.

"I do. Keith told me."

"You've talked to Keith?" Blake asked.

Carson stared at him. "What do you think you're doing, Blake? I know you've seen Keith, so you know damn well that I've talked to him. So, get serious, will you?"

Blake looked away. "Sorry," he mumbled. "Yeah, he stayed here. What about it?"

"He stayed here with you the same night that Hunter Douglas was murdered. Keith fought with Hunter earlier in the evening. I need to know what time he arrived here."

Blake thought for a moment. "I think it was around twelve or so. It was over six months ago, Carson. It's hard to remember the exact time."

"Did Keith stay here the whole night or did he go out again?"

"No. Keith was here with me until he left the next day. He took a shower and went to bed. Well, we talked for a while before that, but he didn't leave until the next day."

"So, Keith was here from around eleven that night until sometime the next day. Is that right?" Carson asked.

"Eleven? I think it was later than that. More like around twelve. Maybe, it was earlier. I'm not sure. As I said, it was a long time ago. But I do remember that he left a little after lunch the next day," Blake replied.

"Which was it? Eleven or twelve?"

Blake shrugged. "I'm not sure. What difference does it make, anyway?"

"What about you? Did you leave the house that night? I mean after Keith arrived. Did you go anywhere after he got to your house?"

"No," Blake said. "I was here with him the whole time."

Carson took his pad out of his pocket and opened it. He flipped through the pages until he found the one he was looking for. "You didn't go outside for any reason?"

"No," Blake said, looking confused. "Why would I?"

"Did you happen to loan your car to anyone that night?"

"Just what are you getting at, Carson? Spit it out, will you?"

"I have reason to believe that you went out after Keith went to bed. I think Keith told you where that party was and what had happened and I think you drove out there looking for Hunter Douglas. I think you waited for him to leave the party, followed him, drove him off the road, and killed him."

Blake stared at him, astonished by what he had just heard. "What the hell have you been smoking, Carson? You have got to be kidding me."

"Your car was moved and parked in a different spot the next morning. If you didn't loan it to someone and you didn't drive it, then, how did it get moved?"

"What the hell are you talking about? My car wasn't moved," Blake yelled.

"I hope to God I'm wrong about this, Blake." He handed him a sheet of folded paper. "This is a search warrant for your car. My men are going through it as we speak. If there's any evidence in it that you killed Hunter Douglas, they'll find it."

Blake sat back in his chair and glared at Carson. "Do I need to call an attorney?"

"You tell me," Carson replied.

Nichole pulled off her gloves and threw her jacket on the small couch. "Brrr," she said, rubbing her hands together. "It's really cold out there. She glanced over at Kari. "How are you feeling today, sweetie? Did you have a good night?"

Nichole walked over to the bed, bent down, and kissed Kari on the forehead. "Can you believe that it's New Year's Eve? I'll be spending it with Keith at home. Of course, he's still not allowed out of the house. Sheriff Katts is confirming that he was with your dad when Hunter was killed. Once that's confirmed, then Keith should be okay."

"However, on the other hand, it's not looking good for your dad," she said. "He has a lot of explaining to do. The police have impounded his car. They found some traces of blood in it and they are checking to see if it belongs to Hunter Douglas. I mean, like, come on police. Seriously? There's no way your dad could have killed Hunter. But I guess they have to check it out to be sure. I feel kind of sorry for your dad. It's horrible to be suspected of something like that."

Kari's leg jerked.

Nichole stared at Kari, waiting to see if it would happen again. It's nothing, she told herself. I should be used to this by now.

Suddenly, Kari's leg jerked again.

"Kari?" Nichole whispered. "What's happening?" As she went to take her daughter's hand, Kari's right index finger started to move.

Just as Nichole jumped off the chair and started towards the door to get help, Betty came running into the room.

"What's happening?" Nichole cried out.

Betty looked over at Nichole. "What did you see?"

"Her leg jerked a couple of times and her finger moved. Her right index finger."

"I need to call Dr. Dunbar and get her over here," Betty said. "I saw a lot of movement on the monitor."

"What's wrong with her eyes?" Nichole exclaimed. Why are they moving like that?"

"Oh, dear God," Betty said. She reached inside the bedside table drawer and pulled out a tongue depressor. Ripping the cellophane off, she stuck the depressor inside Kari's mouth to prevent her from biting her tongue. "She's having a seizure," she told Nichole, as Kari's entire body began to spasm.

"What can I do?" Nichole cried out.

"Go find a doctor."

Nichole stared at her.

"Now!" Betty yelled.

Thirty-one

New Year's Eve

"What are her vitals," Dr. Campbell called out, as he ran into Kari's room.

"She stopped seizing a few seconds ago. Her vitals are almost back to normal," Betty told him. "I don't get it, Dr. Campbell. Why is she getting seizures now? Is this normal?

"No. They usually appear shortly after a person goes into a coma, but there are no hard and fast rules. We're learning more every day about comatose patients. I'm beginning to think that Kari has been having either generalized or myoclonic seizures. They usually only last for seconds and they can cause jerking or spasms."

"Well, I'd say that was a full-blown seizure," Betty declared.

"Is Kari going to be okay?" Nichole asked.

Dr. Campbell glanced over at her, surprised to see her sitting on the couch. Ignoring her, he turned his attention back to Kari. "She seems okay now. I'd like to get her started on Dilantin to see if that will stop any further seizures."

He turned to Nichole. "I'll ask Dr. Dunbar to give you an update."

"Thank you, but can't you at least tell me if she's going to be okay?"

"No, I can't." He turned back to Betty. "I want someone monitoring her for the next few hours. Call me immediately if anything changes. I'll be here until eight."

"Yes, Dr. Campbell," Betty replied.

"Ben, could we . . ."

Without giving Nichole a second look, Ben walked by her and left the room.

"Man, he sure hates you, doesn't he?" Betty remarked.

"I guess. I broke his nose, remember?" Nichole asked.

"Oh, I remember," Betty said, grinning. "But you think he'd get over it. I mean . . . Well, you weren't yourself at the time. You'd think he'd understand that, being a doctor."

"I guess. However, I'm beginning to think he'll never forgive me. I know Dr. Dunbar is a good doctor, but Ben's the best. It doesn't seem fair that Kari is the one who pays the price for something that I did."

"There may be another reason he's distanced himself from you," Betty said.

"Really? And, what would that be?"

"I think he really cared for you."

Nichole stared at her for a moment, then, laughed. "Well, if he did, I sure ruined it, didn't I? Because it's obvious he can't stand the sight of me now."

"There's a fine line between love and hate, you know," Betty said, as she left the room.

Nichole picked up her phone and called Keith. "Hi, honey," she said when he answered. "Kari has had a bad seizure. She's okay now, but I'm going to spend the night here. There's food in the frig if you get hungry."

She listened for a moment. "You, too, honey. Why don't you call some of your friends and ask them over? There's no sense sitting there all by yourself. Call me if you need me, and, Keith, I . . ." Nichole took a deep breath. “I want you to know that I love you very, very much and I’m so happy that you’re back home.”

She waited while Keith answered her. “Whatever you want to do is fine with me. I’ll see you tomorrow. Happy New Year,” she told him.

Nichole sat down beside Kari and took her hand. “It’s just you and me tonight, kiddo. It’s almost the new year. Maybe, with any luck and a lot of praying, this will be the year that you come back to us.”

Thinking he heard pounding on his front door, Blake turned the volume down on the TV and listened. When he heard it again, he got off the couch and went to see who was at the door.

“Blake,” Sheriff Katts, acknowledged, as the door swung open.

“Carson. Now what? A warrant to search my house?” he asked sarcastically.

“Actually, yes,” Carson replied. “And, another one for your arrest.”

“For what!” Blake exclaimed. “I haven’t done anything wrong.”

“We found Hunter Douglas’ blood in your car, Blake. Would you like to explain how it got there?”

Blake took a step back and grabbed onto the wall. “What the hell are you talking about? Is this some kind of a joke?”

“I honestly wish it was. I’m afraid I’m gonna have to take you in, Blake. You’re under arrest for the murder of Hunter Douglas.” Carson turned and motioned to a group of policemen standing behind him on the sidewalk. “Take him in, boys..”

"This sucks, Carson."

"You should probably get your jacket."

"Can I make a phone call first?"

Carson hesitated for a moment, then shook his head no. "You can make your call down at the station."

"I'd like to make it now," Blake said. "Besides, you haven't read me my rights yet." He reached for his phone and hit a speed dial number.

Carson stood back, deciding to allow Blake to make his call.

"Nichole? It's Blake."

"What the . . ?" Carson said, surprised.

"I'm being arrested for Hunter Douglas' murder. Carson is taking me in right now. Can you call your uncle and ask him to meet me there?" He listened to Nichole for a moment. "Of course, I didn't do it," Blake stated emphatically. "Just call him, will you?" Blake put his phone back in his pocket and shrugged. "Well, I guess I better get my jacket."

"You'll need it. It's freezing out there." Carson took a small card out of his shirt pocket and started to inform Blake of his rights. "One moment," he told Blake when his phone rang "Sheriff Katts," he answered. After listening for a few seconds, he grinned. "No, I won't throw the key away."

He listened to the caller and sighed. "I wouldn't be arresting him if I didn't have evidence. And, yes, Keith is free to leave the house, Nichole. However, he's not free to leave town. Got it?"

Sheriff Katts looked at Blake, who was sitting on a chair in the police station, waiting to be processed. "You know what? It's almost seven and I have a New Year's Eve party to go to. I'll talk to you in the morning."

"I told you. I have nothing to talk about."

"Well, there's always the weather," Carson replied, smiling.

"This isn't funny, Carson."

"You're right. It isn't." He looked at Blake, obviously puzzled about something."

"What?" Blake said.

"Why did you do it, Blake? I mean why risk everything now?"

"I'm not talking without my attorney, Carson, so can the questions, will you?"

"Fine," Carson said. "I just don't get it, that's all."

"I told you . . ." Blake looked away. "What happens if my attorney shows up tonight?" Blake asked.

"He'll be allowed to come back to your cell to talk with you," Carson told him.

"But, no bail, right?"

"Not tonight, Blake. Probably tomorrow, if the judge decides to let you out. Whoops. Almost forgot that tomorrow's a holiday. You won't be seeing no judge tomorrow." Carson stood up and stretched. "Well, guess I'll be going. Happy New Year's, Blake," he said, smirking.

"Happy Fuck You, Too, Carson," Blake replied, as he gave him the finger.

Thirty-two

New Year's Day

"Would you like to go to the hospital with me today?"

Keith looked up from the kitchen table and shrugged. "I guess so. But, only for a little while. I don't want to spend the whole day there," he told her.

"That's fine. Do you have anything else on your plate for today?"

"Football, Mom. I plan on eating junk food and watching football all day long."

"Is your driver's license still good?" Nichole asked.

"Yeah, for a few more years. Why?"

"Then, you can take the car home when you're ready to leave the hospital. I'll call you when I'm ready to leave and you can come get me."

Keith smiled. "You're unbelievable," he said.

"I am?" Nichole asked. "Why do you say that?"

"Kari's been in the hospital for over a year and a half and you've been right by her side every single day. You've never stopped talking or reading to her and, more nights than not, you sleep at the hospital. Kari and I are so lucky to have a mom like you."

Nichole bent down and kissed him on top of his head. "It's important that she hears my voice. Anyway, I'm the lucky one," she told him. "There were days when I was so afraid I would never see you again, Keith. Just to have you back home again is so . . ." She wiped a tear from her eye, laughing. "Look at me. Getting all teary-eyed. Sorry. I know how you hate it when I get emotional."

Keith grinned. "That's enough. You'll have me bawling in a minute if you don't stop."

"Do you want any more cereal?"

"No thanks," Keith said. "I'm good for now." He drank the rest of his milk, set the glass down on the table, and burped.

"Really, Keith?" Nichole said.

"Whoops. Excuse me." He sat back and watched Nichole rinse the dishes and put them into the dishwasher. "I've been thinking about going back to school," he declared.

Nichole glanced over at him. "I think that's wonderful, Keith."

"I've missed the last half of my junior year and the first half of my senior year. I figure I can make most of that up during the rest of this school year and over the summer. If I take summer school, that is, and work my butt off, of course."

"I'm impressed," Nichole said. "It looks like you've been thinking about this."

"I have. I'd like to go to college after that and I was wondering if . . ." Keith hesitated.

"If what, dear?"

"Well, I know money is tight with the medical expenses and all and I was wondering if my college fund is still available? I mean, it's okay if you had to spend it. I was just wondering."

"Well, there are always scholarships you can apply for, you know. And . . ."

"That's okay, Mom," Keith interrupted. "I understand."

Nichole smiled. "Let me finish. Your college fund is intact and waiting for you. Your grandparents set it up for you and it's all there. However, I would encourage you to apply for as many scholarships as possible."

Keith grinned. "Are you serious? The money's still available?"

"I'm serious. There is no way your grandparents would have spent that money. And, talking about your grandparents, I have more news for you."

Keith looked at her, waiting.

"They are buying you a car," Nichole told him.

"No way!" Keith shouted. "A car? Really?"

"Not a new one, you understand, but your grandfather knows someone who sells used cars and he mentioned that he was going to buy one for you. You're not supposed to know, though, so you have to act surprised when he tells you."

"Is he going to let me pick it out?" Keith asked. "I mean, if he picks it out, it will be an old man's car."

"When I talked to your grandfather, he said he was going to call you sometime today to make plans with you up so you can pick – out – your – car."

"Yes!"

"And, remember, it's a surprise."

Keith jumped up and hugged his mother. "You're the best," he exclaimed.

"I think you mean your grandfather, Keith."

"No. I mean you, Mom."

Nichole looked at the kitchen clock to check the time. "We better get going."

"Mom?"

"Yes, dear."

"Do you think dad killed Hunter Douglas?"

Nichole shook her head no. "Your dad doesn't have it in him, Keith. Never in a million years will I believe he is capable of doing something like that."

"I'm not so sure," Keith commented.

"What are you talking about? That's a horrible thing to say about your dad."

"You're right. Never mind. I'm sorry I brought it up."

"Why did you say that?"

"Forget it, Mom. I didn't mean it."

"Keith?"

"I'm gonna grab my jacket. I left it upstairs. I'll be ready in a minute."

Nichole watched as her son ran out of the room. What the hell was that all about, she wondered, making a mental note to ask him again what he was referring to.

Thirty-three

"How can you possibly know that?" Keith asked his mother, as they stepped off the elevator and headed towards Kari's room.

"Nichole, hold up a minute."

Nichole turned to see Betty walking towards her and Keith. "Happy New Year, Betty. What's up?"

"Happy New Year. Dr. Dunbar would like to talk to you before you go in to see Kari. Would you mind waiting out here? She'll be with you in a minute."

"What's going on, Betty?" Nichole stared at Betty, trying to discern if the nurse was concerned or upset about something.

"It's good to see you, Keith," Betty said, ignoring Nichole. "What's going on with you today? Any special plans?"

"Nah. Just going to watch some football."

"Well, it is the day for it," Betty commented. "Ah, here's Dr. Dunbar now," she remarked, as the door to Kari's room opened and the doctor walked out.

Nichole stepped forward to greet the doctor and shook her hand. "Good morning. What's going on, Dr. Dunbar."

"Good morning, Nichole. Let's sit over here for a moment, shall we?"

"You're scaring me, Doctor. Has something happened to Kari?"

"Yes, and it's good news." Dr. Dunbar took Nichole's hand and held it. "Kari has regained . . ." she hesitated. "Kari woke up," she said, smiling.

Nichole stared at her, shocked at what she thought she had just heard. "She's awake? Did you just say she's awake? Oh, my, God, Keith," Nichole said, reaching for her son's hand. "Kari is awake."

Keith, grinning from ear to ear, hugged his mother. "Well, it's about time," he exclaimed. "Let's go say hi."

"Hold on," Dr. Dunbar instructed, as Keith made a move toward Kari's room. "There are a few things you need to know before you go in there."

"What are they?" Nichole asked as she stood up, anxious to see her daughter.

"She's in and out," Dr. Dunbar stated. "She wakes up for a few minutes and then drifts off to sleep. Note that I said sleep. When she is awake, she is confused, which is normal. It usually takes a while before a patient can understand what is going on. And, you need to remember that she has lost over a year and a half of her life. The last thing she remembers is going to her senior prom."

"I understand," Nichole said. "We are to treat her with kid gloves."

"Correct. Wait for her to ask the questions and, then, answer them. Don't pressure her and try to get her to remember stuff. It won't work. She is going to need a lot of physical and mental therapy. She can't walk at this point."

"How is she mentally? You said she remembered her prom. Does she remember the accident?"

"I don't think so," Dr. Dunbar told her. "But, at this point, we're asking her simple things. Like what is two times two, who is the president, or does she remember how to spell her name? Simple things. What you have to remember is that her recovery could take months – even years, Mrs. Armstrong."

"Years?" Keith exclaimed. "So, when will she be able to come home?"

Dr. Dunbar looked at Keith and smiled. "I know you'd like to see your sister back home, but that's not going to happen for a while. You are going to have to be patient."

"Will Kari be able to stay here during her recovery?" Nichole asked.

"Let's talk about that later, shall we? Now, would you like to say hello to Kari?"

"I'm nervous," Nichole declared, as she took Keith's hand and squeezed it.

"Is she sleeping?" Keith asked as they entered Kari's room.

"Kari?" Dr. Dunbar said softly. "Are you awake, dear?"

Kari slowly opened her eyes and looked towards the door. "Where's dad?"

"I'm not talking to you until my attorney gets here," Blake said. "I know my rights."

"Good for you," Carson replied as he sat down across from Blake. "However, I'm here as your friend this morning, Blake."

Blake looked over at him and shook his head. "I doubt that very much, Carson. We stopped being friends a long time ago."

"I know you feel that way and I'm sorry. However, this is about Kari."

Blake's whole body stiffened up, as he leaned forward in his chair. "Has something happened to Kari?" he exclaimed. "Tell me, for God's sake."

"Easy, Blake. It's good news. Kari woke up early this morning. Nichole called and asked me to tell you. Kari asked for you, Blake."

"Oh, dear God," Blake cried out, as the tears ran down his cheeks. "My baby girl is awake," he sobbed. "Kari's awake, Carson."

"I know," Carson said, smiling.

"Can I . . . Can I . . ." He put his head in his hands and sobbed.

"I'm going to let you see her," Carson said. "I checked with her doctor and she said I could take you over around three this afternoon to see her."

Blake looked at Carson through his tears and smiled. "Thank you."

"Now, pull yourself together. I still have a bunch of questions for you regarding the Douglas kid."

"Not without my attorney, you don't," Blake replied as he wiped the tears away from his eyes.

"Let me explain something to you," Carson said. "You don't have to talk. Just listen. We have enough evidence right now to convict you of murdering Hunter Douglas. The night Hunter was murdered, your car was moved sometime between eleven-thirty and seven the next morning."

"How do you . . ."

Carson held up his hand. "Stop. Just listen to me. I know this because Keith told me."

Blake stared at him. "No way he said that," he said angrily. "Keith would never have said that."

"I'm sorry, Blake. But, he did. Which, of course, led to the search of your car, where we discovered traces of Hunter's blood and the knife you used to kill him."

"You found what?" Blake screamed.

"I don't understand how you could have been so careless as to leave the knife in your car, Blake. What the hell were you thinking?"

Blake stared at him. "No! This is all wrong. I didn't kill that kid. God knows I had a reason, but I didn't touch him. This is messed up, Carson." He stared at the sheriff for a few moments. "It was you!" he yelled. "You planted that blood and knife there."

"And, why would I do that? No, Blake. No one planted anything. You left the house after Keith had gone to sleep and drove out to the Williams' house. You waited for Hunter to leave the party, you followed him, drove him off the road, and killed him. Plain and simple. You did it."

"You are so far off base . . ."

"Sorry, my friend, but I am arresting you for the murder of Hunter Douglas."

Blake glared at him. "You asshole. You did that already."

"I did, didn't I? However, I don't think I finished reading you your rights." Carson walked over to the door and opened it. He glanced around, spotted a uniformed cop, and yelled at him to come over.

"Do you need something, Sheriff?"

"Officer O'Reilly, please read Mr. Armstrong his rights and put him back in his cell."

"Yes, Sir."

“Are you still going to take me to see Kari this afternoon?” Blake yelled at Carson.

Carson turned and looked at him. “We’ll see,” he said smiling.

Thirty-four

"That's it," Dr. Dunbar declared. "You need to leave. Kari needs her rest."

"But we've only been here for fifteen minutes. I'm not ready to leave," Nichole stated. "I want to stay with her a little longer."

"I understand how you feel, Mrs. Armstrong, but it isn't a good idea for family members to be here for long periods of time. It can cause too much stress on the patient."

"But I've waited . . ."

"I understand what you've gone through," Dr. Dunbar interrupted, "but, for the next few weeks, your visits will be limited to fifteen minutes twice a day. Kari is going to be closely monitored twenty-four-seven, so you don't have to be concerned about her."

"That doesn't seem fair," Keith said. "My mom has been at Kari's side every day since her accident and she should be allowed to stay here with her."

"I'm sorry, but Kari will be going through a lot in the weeks to come. We want to start her physical therapy as soon as possible. A neurologist will be testing her to determine if there has been any or how much brain deterioration. I've talked to Kari a few times and it's obvious she will need help with her speech. She has trouble remembering words and we need to help her with that. If your mother is here all the time – well, to put it bluntly, Keith – she will be in the way."

"I'll be in the way?" Nichole shouted. "I'm her mother and I . . ."

"This is exactly what I'm talking about," Dr. Dunbar interrupted. "These kinds of outbursts aren't going to do Kari any good. Now, if you'll excuse me, I've got work to do and you need to leave."

"I'm not going . . ."

"Come on, Mom," Keith said, taking his mother's arm. "We can get this straightened out later. Getting upset isn't going to help anything." He looked over at Dr. Dunbar. "Can you tell us when we are allowed back to see Kari?"

"You need to talk to Betty. You know, she's the nurse who . . ."

"I know who she is. I've only seen her every day for almost two years," Nichole said sarcastically.

"She has a schedule to give you with the appointment times you can visit."

Nichole shook her head in disgust. "I can't frickin' believe this shit," she muttered.

"Mrs. Armstrong, don't start up with me. It's this or nothing."

"Come on, Keith, let's get out of here." Nichole grabbed her son's arm and walked out of the room.

"You shouldn't get so upset, Mom. It's not good for you," Keith declared, as they walked down the hall toward the elevator.

"I don't know who that doctor thinks she is, but we'll see what she's got to say after Uncle Andrew gets done with her."

"Nichole, wait," Betty said loudly as Nichole walked past the nurse's station.

Nichole turned and looked at her. "What?"

"How did it go in there?" Betty asked.

"The doctor is an ass," Nichole said. "I'd like to know whose bright idea it was to only allow me to see Kari for thirty minutes a day."

"I'm sorry about that," Betty said. "I should have warned you before you went into Kari's room. But you know I could get into trouble . . ."

"Forget it. It's not your fault," Nichole said. "So, I guess I need a copy of the schedule before I leave."

"Here it is," Betty said as she handed Nichole a sheet of paper.

"Thanks," she said as she glanced at the paper. "No way in hell!" she exclaimed.

"What is it?" Keith asked.

"Your father is on this list to see Kari at three o'clock."

"What's wrong with that?" Keith asked her.

"Betty? Why is Blake on this list?" Nichole asked.

Betty shrugged. "I was told to add him."

"By who? Who told you to add him?"

"Dr. Dunbar. She said that Sheriff Katts was going to bring him over to see Kari at three o'clock."

"Why would Sheriff Katts be bringing Blake here? I don't understand what's going on."

Betty stared at her with a surprised look. "You don't know?"

"Know what?" Nichole exclaimed. "What the hell is going on, Betty?"

"I'm sorry, but Mr. Armstrong has been arrested for the murder of Hunter Douglas."

"You've got fifteen minutes, Blake. And you better make the best of them, because it will probably be a long time before you see your daughter again," Carson said.

Blake stood in the doorway of Kari's room and stared at his daughter. "She looks like she's sleeping," Blake said. He turned and looked at Betty. "Can I wake her?"

Betty smiled. "I think she is awake," she told him. She walked over to the side of Kari's bed and bent down. "Kari? Your dad is here. Are you awake?" she asked in a soft voice.

"Too bright," Kari mumbled.

"Keith, pull the blinds, will you?" Betty asked.

Keith walked over to the large window, pulled down the blinds, and closed the curtains.

"How's that?" Betty asked.

Very slowly Kari opened her eyes and looked at her father. "Hi, Dad."

"Hi, baby girl," Blake said, tears filling his eyes. "About time you woke up. I've missed you."

"Did you, Dad?" She glanced over at Sheriff Katts and smiled. "I know you," she commented. "You're Coach Katts."

"That's right, Kari. How are you doing?"

Kari smiled. "They say I'm a miracle."

"You certainly are," Carson replied.

"Mom was here a lot," Kari stated. "I could hear her."

"Is that right?" Blake asked.

"I dreamed I saw Keith," Kari declared as she shut her eyes. "I'm tired. You can go now."

"I've still got a few minutes, honey."

Kari didn't say anything.

"She's asleep," Betty said.

"That fast?" Blake asked.

"She drifts in and out. The problem she's having now is that she has short-term memory loss. I doubt she'll remember you were here," Betty told Blake.

"But she remembers things that she heard while she was in a coma?"

"It seems so," Betty replied. "Not everything, of course, but she's mentioned some of the things she heard."

Carson put his hand on Blake's shoulder and grinned. "No kidding. Well, here's hoping that you get lucky," he said.

"What do you mean by that?" Blake asked.

"Just that you better hope that she doesn't remember that you wanted to pull the plug."

Thirty-five

Nichole pulled her car into the driveway, put it into park, and turned the engine off. She glanced at a car that was parked in front of her house but she didn't recognize it. She got out of her car, walked to the front door, and went inside. As Nichole closed the front door, she was surprised to hear Keith talking to someone in the kitchen. She hesitated when she heard the name Hunter mentioned.

"That fucker didn't know what hit him."

Keith laughed. "He thought he was so tough. I guess we showed him."

"He bled a lot, didn't he?"

"You idiot. Of course, he bled a lot. That's what happens when you stab someone."

"What do you think is going to happen to your dad?"

"I don't know and I couldn't care less."

"You really hate him, don't you?"

"Hey, better him than me rotting away in some jail. At least the cops will close the case on Hunter's murder and that will be the end of it."

Nichole stood still, shocked at what she had just heard. Although her first instinct told her to get the hell out of the house, she took a deep breath, trying to pull herself together. She opened the front door, waited for a second, and, then, slammed it shut. "Hi, Keith. I'm home," she called out.

"I'm in the kitchen," Keith called back. "Come see who is here."

Nichole walked into the kitchen and looked over at Jason. “Well, I’ll be,” she said. “Jason Krueger. It’s been years since I’ve seen you.”

“How are you, Mrs. Armstrong?” Jason asked.

“I thought you were in jail.”

“I was, but the only thing they could hold me on was failure to appear for a court date. So, now I’ve got another court date and they let me out until then. My mom posted bail, so I’m good for a while.”

“It all gets a little confusing, doesn’t it, Jason?” Nichole said smiling. “So, I must say that I’m surprised to see you two together, Keith, after what Jason did to you.”

“What did Jason do?” Keith asked, looking confused.

“Well, if I remember correctly, he told Sheriff Katts that you killed Hunter Douglas. Or, have you forgotten that already, Keith?”

“Oh, that,” Keith said, laughing. “He was just messing with Katts.”

“I don’t find that funny at all. You could be in jail right now for murdering Hunter.”

“There was never a chance of that, Mrs. A. I knew Keith didn’t do it. After all, Hunter was killed way after I dropped Keith off at his dad’s. Right, Keith?”

“Right. Geez, Mom, don’t be so serious.”

“I see. Well, I still don’t like what you did, Jason. So, what are you two up to?

“Just chewing the fat,” Keith said. “Jason was just about to leave.”

“Are you driving back to Milwaukee tonight?” Nichole asked.

"Tomorrow. I'm gonna stay with a friend here tonight."

"Well, it was nice seeing you again, Jason. Have a safe trip home," Nichole told him, as she started to leave the kitchen

"Nice seeing you, too, Mrs. A," Jason replied.

Nichole walked out of the kitchen, wavering between going upstairs or eavesdropping on the boys.

"Well, I guess I'll leave," Jason said loudly.

"Yeah, give me a call."

"Will do," Jason replied.

Nichole waited.

"Do you think your mom heard anything?" Jason asked, whispering.

"Nah. No sweat. Don't worry about it."

Nichole barely made it to her bedroom before her knees gave out. She dropped to the floor, her whole body shaking. *I've got to call Carson, she thought. No. No. I can't do that. I can't turn Keith in.* As she started to get off the floor, Keith walked into the room.

"Are you hurt?" he asked. "What happened?"

"No. I'm fine," Nichole told him. "Well, actually, I twisted my ankle and I wasn't sure if I should put any weight on it."

"Let me help you up," Keith said, as he reached down and took her arm. He pulled Nichole up off the floor and helped her to the bed. "Can I get you anything? Do you want some ice?"

Nichole forced herself to smile. "I'm fine, sweetie. I think I'll just rest here for a few minutes."

"You sure?" Keith asked.

"I'm sure."

"You aren't upset because Jason came over, are you?"

"Of course not. You can have your friends over any time you want."

"Thanks."

"No thanks are necessary. This is your house, too, Keith."

"I'm gonna go watch some TV. You try to get some rest, okay?" Keith said as he walked towards the door. "By the way, are you going to the hospital tonight?"

"Yes, and tonight, according to the schedule, I can see Kari between eight-thirty and eight-forty-five. This is such a bunch of bullshit, Keith. Kari's been out of her coma for three days now and each one of my visits has been at a different time."

"I know, but maybe Uncle Andrew will take care of that for you."

"I can only hope."

"Sheriff Katts."

"Carson, this is Nichole."

Carson grinned. "How are you, Nichole? Missing me?"

"Get serious, will you?"

"Just joking," Carson said. "What can I do for you, Nichole?"

"I need to talk to you. It's about Blake and it's important."

"I was just on my way home. Can it wait until tomorrow?"

"Mom?"

Nichole turned and saw Keith standing in the doorway of her bedroom, listening to her conversation. She held up a finger indicating he should wait a moment. "Tomorrow is fine," she told Carson. "I'll call you in the morning. Goodnight."

"You know that it isn't polite to listen in on a person's conversation," she said, as she ended the call.

Keith laughed. "You should practice what you preach, Mom."

"Exactly what is that supposed to mean?"

"I know that you were eavesdropping on Jason and me."

"I was not."

"Don't lie, Mom. It isn't nice. Was that Coach Katts you were talking to just now?"

"It was."

"Why were you calling him, Mom?"

"I wanted to find out if your father was going to see Kari again, that's all," Nichole said.

"Your face is turning red, Mom. I know you're lying to me."

"Don't be silly, Keith. There's no reason for me to lie to you. I'll be leaving for the hospital in a little while. Do you want to go with me?" Nichole asked.

Keith stared at his mother. "Just how much of Jason's and my conversation did you hear before you came into the kitchen?"

"What are you talking about? I didn't hear any of your conversation. Why? Is there something you don't want me to know?"

"How's your ankle?" Keith asked, suddenly changing the subject. "Maybe you should stay home tonight."

"My ankle feels fine, thank you."

"Isn't it a little early to leave for the hospital?"

"That's enough, Keith. I don't know what's going on in that head of yours but just stop it right now. I don't like you giving me the third degree and I don't like the way you're acting," Nichole yelled.

"Whoa!" Keith cried out, taking a couple of steps backward. "Where did that come from?"

"This is crazy," Nichole said. "I'm leaving and I hope that by the time I get home, you'll be back to your normal self."

"Whatever that is," Keith joked.

Nichole stared at him. "What is going on with you? You're scaring me, Keith."

"Sorry, Mom, I didn't mean to upset you."

"Well, you did." She forced herself to smile. "Let's just forget it. I guess everyone is on edge these days. Anyway, I'm going to stop and pick up some groceries on my way home. Is there anything special you'd like?"

"I think we're out of popcorn."

"I'll pick some up."

"And, Mom?"

"Yes, Keith."

"I don't think it's a good idea for you to talk to Sheriff Katts again. After all, he did arrest dad."

"I don't . . ."

"You know that dad thinks the sheriff planted that evidence, Mom," Keith interrupted. "And, well, he still is my dad and I love him no matter what he did. So, maybe it would be best if you stay away from the sheriff. Okay?"

Nichole felt a chill run through her body as Keith talked. She shook her head yes. “Of course, Keith Whatever you want. No big deal.”

“Thanks, Mom. I think it’s for the best.”

Thirty-six

Sheriff Katts turned and looked up as he felt a hand touch his shoulder. He smiled when he saw it was Nichole. "You're late," he told her, as she slid into the booth across from him.

"Sorry. I actually caught Kari awake and took advantage of not being monitored while we talked."

"How's she doing?" Carson asked.

"Pretty good. She still has short-term memory loss, but the doctors say that will get better."

"Coffee?" Carson asked.

"Please. And, I can't stay long. Keith will want to know where I was."

"Really?" Carson said, grinning. "Since when do you answer to him? Or, anyone else for that matter."

"Since this afternoon. He thinks, but he isn't sure, that I overheard him and Jason Krueger talking in my kitchen."

"Krueger was there? That's not good. Anyway, what's the big deal if you did overhear them talking?"

"They were talking about Hunter Douglas, Carson. I'm pretty sure that Keith and Jason killed him and Keith planted the evidence in Blake's car."

Carson sat back in his seat and stared at Nichole. "No way! Why in the world would he do that to his own father? No. I don't believe it."

"Then, tell me, why I'm afraid to go home and be alone with my son? He overheard me talking to you on the phone and he told me to stay away from you. He pretty much ordered me not to talk to you again. I heard him and Jason talking about how much blood there was after Hunter was stabbed. I'm not making this up, for God's sake. I'm afraid."

Carson watched her carefully as she spoke. He finished off his coffee and looked over at her. "Nichole, none of this makes sense. You know that I know you had some problems in the past and you went a little crazy. I'm talking about that PMS shit or menopause or whatever it was that caused it. Are you sure this isn't happening again and that you're exaggerating what you think you heard?"

"No, it's not happening again. And, you're the one person I thought would understand," Nichole said. "Keith is not the same person he was before he ran away. He's been way too nice, promising to finish school and go on to college and, then, not making any attempt at all."

"First of all, he's only been back a few days, Nichole, and school has been closed for the holidays. And, second - well you're complaining about him being too nice? Most parents would be happy to have a nice child."

"I know that and I can't explain what I mean. But, he's different. At first, I bought it, but I think it's all been a big act for my benefit. And, Jason Krueger is no angel. The two of them were into some bad shit while Keith was gone, Carson. Keith promised me that he wasn't going to see Jason again. The very fact that they are still hanging out with each other – well, I think that same crap is going on."

"And, you think the two of them killed Douglas?"

"I do. I think they got high and got stupid."

"All right. Say they did do it. What do you want me to do about it? All I have to go on is your word – better known as hearsay. Where's your evidence, Nichole? I can't just let Blake out of jail. Or, throw Keith in, for that matter. I'm sorry."

"I know," Nichole whispered.

"I'm surprised you even told me about this. There aren't many mothers who would turn their kid over to the cops. Especially, so their ex could be set free. I'd think you'd be happy to see Blake sitting in prison for the rest of his life."

Nichole stared at him. "You're an ass, Carson. I may not like Blake very much, but I don't want to see him punished for something he didn't do. And, Keith needs help. It's pretty obvious that somehow his wires got crossed. And, when a mother reaches the point where she is afraid of what her son may do to her, she does something about it. I'm not going back into that house knowing that I might end up like Hunter Douglas."

"Are you actually that afraid?"

"What do you think I've been trying to tell you? I heard them talking about killing Hunter. My son is a murderer. For God's sake, how do you think that makes me feel?" Nichole asked as she fought to hold back her tears.

"Okay, I get it," Carson told her. "I believe you, but that doesn't change anything. There still isn't anything I can do about it."

"I see. Well, then, I'm sorry I wasted your time."

"You didn't waste my time and I'm glad you called me. Why don't we both sleep on this and I'll look into it in the morning? Perhaps, we missed something that will put Keith and Jason at the crime scene. Do you think you'll be okay to spend the night at home? Maybe you should spend the night in a motel."

"You know what, Carson? I'm going to tell Keith that I spoke to you about Blake. If he knows I spent time with you tonight he'll be angry, especially after he told me not to talk to you. However, I don't think anything will happen tonight." Nichole shrugged. "At least, I hope not. I guess we'll find out, won't we?"

"Are you sure about this?"

"Just call me in the morning, will you? If I don't answer . . ."

"You'll be fine."

"Will I, Carson?"

"Where have you been, Mom?" Keith asked as Nichole walked into her house. "Your fifteen minutes with Kari were over a long time ago."

Nichole took off her winter coat and hung it up. She glanced into the living room and looked at Keith. "I'll be right back," she told him. "I want a beer."

"It's all gone," Keith said. "We finished it."

"We? Who is we?"

"Jason and me," Keith told her.

"I thought he went to a friend's house?"

"He came back."

"It looks like you two are pretty friendly."

"I guess. After all, I did stay with him and his mom for quite a while. So, yeah, I guess you can say we're friends."

"We sure are, Mrs. A," Jason said, coming up behind her.

Nichole jumped. "You ass! You scared the hell out of me!" she shouted.

"You should have seen the look on your face," Keith said, laughing. "Right, Jason?"

"She jumped like a scared rabbit," Jason replied, grinning.

"That wasn't funny," Nichole said, obviously shaken up.

"Come sit down, Mom," Keith said. "We need to ask you a question."

"I don't think so, Keith. I'm tired and I'm going to bed. Whatever you want to talk about can wait until tomorrow."

"Come on, Mom. It's just one little question."

"Well, maybe two," Jason added. "I've got a question for your mom, Keith."

"That's enough, you two. I'm not in the mood." Nichole turned and started walking to the stairs.

"How is Kari doing?" Jason asked, smirking. "I've been thinking about visiting her."

Nichole turned back and stared at Jason. "You will do no such thing," she told him. "You stay away from Kari."

"Or, what?" Jason asked.

Nichole looked at Keith, waiting for him to say something. "Keith?" she finally said.

"Mom, you know I love you and all, but I told you to stay away from Coach Katts."

"And, I don't take orders from you."

"Well, you see, Mom, this is what you don't seem to understand. When I tell you to do something, you need to listen to me."

Nichole felt a chill go through her body. She gathered up her courage and glared at Keith. "I think you're forgetting who the parent is here, Keith. You don't tell me what to do."

Keith shook his head. "No. You don't get it. We know you eavesdropped on us while we were in the kitchen. We know what you heard."

"Keith, I have no idea what you are referring to. I told you I did not eavesdrop on your conversation."

"You're lying again. Anyway, Jason and I have talked this over."

"Talked what over?"

"What to do with you, of course."

"What to do . . ." Nichole stepped back into the entry and glanced over at the door.

"Don't even think about leaving, Mrs. A," Jason said.

"Here's the deal, Mom," Keith said. "You tell Coach Katts you made a mistake about what you thought you heard and Jason won't go visit Kari at the hospital."

"You wouldn't," Nichole murmured, as she tried to control her body from shaking.

Keith grinned maliciously. "I'm afraid that Jason would. By the way, he followed you, Mom. I told you to stay away from Katts, Mom.

"Why, Keith? For God's sake, just give me a reason why you did it. Revenge for Kari after all this time? It doesn't make sense. The accident was so long ago."

"See, Jason, I told you she heard us," Keith said, grinning.

"How about that? You were right. I wasn't really sure she had been listening until now," Jason said.

"Keith, listen to me. You need help. Turn yourself in now. Sheriff Katts said he would do whatever he can to make sure you get the help you need. Please, Keith. You can't let your father spend the rest of his life in prison for something you did."

"Why not? He doesn't care about me, just like he doesn't care about Kari. He wanted to let her die. Remember all the fights you had, Mom? Kari would be dead right now if he had gotten his way."

"Yes, but I fought him and won and she's not dead and she will need us to take care of her when she comes home," Nichole exclaimed.

Keith stared at her. "That's right. But, how can I take care of her if I'm in jail or . . ." He laughed. "In a looney bin?"

"But, if you get some help, you'll be able to come home one day," Nichole said.

Keith shook his head no. "I really don't care for that idea. You know, turning myself in. You need to call Sheriff Katts and tell him you were wrong."

"I don't think I can do that, Keith."

"Mom doesn't think she can do that, Jason. Did you hear me give her a choice? I don't remember saying if you please, do you?"

"Mrs. A, I really think you should listen to Keith and call Sheriff Katts."

"Or, what?"

"I don't think you want to find out."

Thirty-seven

"Who was that, dear?" Missy asked her husband.

"Nobody," Carson told her.

"Well, it must have been someone. Is there a problem at the station?"

"It's nothing," Carson said.

Missy stared at her husband, wondering what was wrong. "It's something," she said after a few moments. "I know when something is bothering you."

"That was Nichole Armstrong. I talked to her earlier tonight about Keith. She's worried that he might have done something wrong and she wanted my advice. Now, she just told me that she was mistaken and everything is fine."

"What does your gut say?"

Carson grinned. "That I could use a snack before I go back to sleep. Is there any of that pie left?"

"Don't be changing the subject, Carson. You're worried about her, aren't you?"

"A little, but she sounded all right on the phone. You never know with her one way or the other. I'll give her a call in the morning to make sure she's okay."

"Well, she did have that episode a while back when she went a little crazy. Maybe, she's not over it."

"No, that's not it." Carson sat down on the edge of the bed and let out a sigh. "She seemed pretty concerned when I talked to her earlier. Maybe, I should drive over there and make sure she's okay."

"It's late and you need your sleep. Can't it wait until morning?"

"I guess," he said. "But first I'm having a piece of that pie."

"Not a good idea, Carson," Missy said.

"Can I bring you a piece?" he asked as he walked out of the room and headed for the kitchen.

"Who are you calling this early in the morning?" Missy asked as she poured Carson a cup of coffee.

"Nichole Armstrong. I'm concerned about her."

"She's probably still in bed," Missy stated, as Carson held up a finger indicating she should be quiet.

"Good morning," Carson said. "I need to speak to your mother. Put her on the phone." He listened for a moment, frowning. "I see. It's kind of early for her to be there, isn't it?" He shook his head, as Keith answered his question. "All right. When you talk to her, will you please let her know I need to talk to her?"

Carson ended his call and sat back in his chair. "Somethings wrong," he told Missy.

"I gather Nichole wasn't there," Missy stated.

"Keith answered her cell phone. He says she forgot it and that she's at the hospital. There is no way Nichole would forget her phone and it's way too early for her to be visiting Nichole."

"It does seem a little strange," Missy agreed. She stared at Carson.

"What?"

"May I ask why you have Nichole's phone number in your phone? That seems a little strange, too."

Carson smiled. "Really, Missy? Isn't it a little early in the morning for you to bring out your jealous gene?"

Missy grinned. “Well, you know me. I just can’t help it.”

“She called me last night, if you remember. That’s why I have her number in my phone.” Carson stood up and stretched. “Anyway, you should know by now that you have nothing to worry about.” He bent down and kissed her.” You know you’re the only one I’ve ever had eyes for. And, I’ve got to get going. I’ll call you later.”

“Bye,” Missy called out as Carson opened the door to leave. “Love you.”

“Love you, too,” Carson said, shutting the door behind him.

Sheriff Katts exited the elevator and walked down the hallway toward Kari’s room. He pushed open the door and looked inside. Kari was curled up like a little ball, sleeping. The bathroom door was open and the light was off. Obviously, Kari was alone in the room. He turned and walked back to the nurse’s station and looked around.

“Can I help you?”

Surprised, Carson turned to see a young man dressed in white standing behind him. “Where did you come from?”

The man smiled. “It’s the shoes. They don’t make any noise at all. It seems I’m always startling people. Anyway, I was in the room behind us. Can I help you with something?”

“I’m Sheriff Katts. I’d like to know if Kari Armstrong has had any visitors this morning?”

“Not that I’m aware of. Besides, it’s too early for visitors.”

"Actually, it's her mother I'm looking for. Do you know if Mrs. Armstrong was here this morning?"

"Not that I'm aware of. I'm pretty sure that no one has been here to see Kari." He walked around the counter and looked down at a sheet of paper. "It says here that Kari's mom isn't due to visit her until eleven this morning."

"I guess I got some bad information. I'm sorry to have bothered you."

"No bother at all, Detective."

"Sheriff," Katts corrected him. "And, it's Sheriff Katts, not Detective."

"Sorry."

Katts thought for a moment. "Would you give me a call when Mrs. Armstrong shows up? I'll give you my number so you can call me directly."

"I'm sorry, but my shift is about to end. However, I can leave a note for whoever is working to call you. How's that?"

"That's fine. Thanks."

As Carson pulled away from the front of the hospital, he glanced over at the almost empty parking lot. Noticing a car that was similar to Nichole's, he pulled into the lot and drove over to the car. He stopped, got out of his car, and looked inside. He tried to open the door but it was locked. Checking the license plate, he ran the number through the computer to confirm who owned the car. The computer verified that the car belonged to Nichole. "Damn! I guess it's time to go talk to Keith," he uttered, as he drove away.

Sheriff Katts pounded on the front door and waited. A few moments later, the door swung open.

"What?"

"Jason Krueger," Katts said surprised. "What are you doing here?"

"What do you want?" Jason asked again.

"I want to talk to Keith. Where is he?"

Jason turned towards the stairs and yelled, "Hey, Keith, the cops are here. Run for it!"

"Very funny," Keith said, as he came down the stairs. He looked at Katts and frowned. "It's kind of early for a visit, isn't it Coach."

"Good morning and for right now it's Sheriff Katts, not Coach."

"Right."

"We need to talk, Keith."

Keith yawned and motioned to the living room. "Let's go sit down."

"You look like you had a rough night." Katts glanced over at Jason. "You, too," he declared.

"We were up late," Keith said. "What do you want?"

"Your mother isn't at the hospital. Her car is there, but she never saw Kari."

"I know," Keith told him. "She called me."

"She called you?" He looked over at Jason, who was standing in the doorway listening to the conversation. "Take a seat," he told Jason.

"I'm fine right here," Jason replied.

"I'm not asking you. Sit down, Jason."

Jason hesitated a moment, then, sighed. "Fine," he muttered, giving Katts a dirty look. He walked over to the couch and plopped down. "Happy now?" he muttered.

Ignoring him, Katts turned his attention back to Keith. "What's going on here? Where's your mom?"

"All I know is that she called and said that her car pooped out in the hospital parking lot. She said she was going to call someone to come out and take a look at it."

"You have her phone, so where did she call from?"

"She used a phone in the hospital."

"I was told she wasn't there this morning. How do you explain that?"

Keith shrugged. "I don't know. I guess she called from the registration desk. It's on the first floor right when you enter the hospital. Anyhow she said she was probably going to have to rent a car and she'd be home later."

"And, she was okay with him spending the night here?" Katts asked, looking over at Jason.

"She was fine with it. Why shouldn't she be?"

"Yeah, man," Jason interjected. "She was fine with it. She likes me, you know?"

"Right. Because you're such a loveable person."

"You got it, man," Jason replied, grinning.

Katts stood up and looked at the two young men. "Call me if you hear from your mom again, Keith."

"All right," Keith said.

Katts walked to the front door and opened it. "By the way, Keith, you may have been wrong about your dad moving the car the night Hunter Douglas was murdered."

Keith stared at him. "Really?" he said after a few moments.

“Yep. It looks like he never left the house at all that night. Guess our killer is still out there.”

Thirty-eight

"Mikey, I want you to go over to the hospital and look at the surveillance tapes from last Tuesday."

Deputy Truhouse looked up at Sheriff Katts, who was standing in front of his desk. "What am I looking for?"

"Nichole Armstrong parked her car there sometime between late Monday night and early Tuesday morning. See if you can find her on the tapes and what she's doing. Her kid says she drove over early to see Kari, but she never made it to Kari's room. I need to know if she ever entered the hospital and, if she did, how long she was in there."

"Got it," Truhouse said as he got off his chair and headed towards the door.

"Wait. I'm not finished," Katts said. "Also, check through the tapes from Wednesday and Thursday. I want to find out when her car left the parking lot. According to Keith, Nichole called a repair shop on Tuesday morning and asked if someone could come out and take a look at it. I've checked around and none of the repair shops around here recall getting a phone call from her. We need to find that car."

"Okay," Truhouse said, as he stared at Katts.

"What are you waiting for?" Katts asked.

"I just want to be sure you're done, that's all," Truhouse said, smiling.

"Seriously?" Katts asked, shaking his head. "Get out of here."

"See you later," Truhouse told him, waving as he left the room.

Blake Armstrong wasn't talking. His attorney had told him to keep his mouth shut and that was exactly what he intended to do. So, when Sheriff Katts walked into the room and greeted him, Blake kept quiet.

Carson grinned. "Not even a hello, Blake?"

Blake stared at him.

"Okay, then I'll talk and you listen. Nichole has been missing for three days."

Blake's head jerked up and he stared at Carson.

"That got your attention, didn't it?" Carson said, grinning. "Now, we have spent quite a few hours looking at surveillance tapes from the hospital."

Carson looked over at Blake, who was staring at him. "You want to say anything?"

"You aren't going to pin this one on me, too, Carson."

Carson gave him a nasty look. "Don't be a smart ass. And, I didn't pin anything on you." He took a sip of coffee and smacked his lips. "Good coffee. Now, the tapes show Nichole parking her car and walking into the hospital around five in the morning. The strange thing is, we haven't found any video of her leaving, but her car is gone and we don't know exactly when it was moved or by whom."

"Don't the tapes show who took it?" Blake asked.

"If they do, we haven't found it yet," Carson replied. "I called to have the car towed to our impound lot. The driver didn't show up until Thursday, for some dumb ass reason, and her car was gone."

"So, it just magically vanished," Blake commented.

"Seems like it. Anyway, we know that after Nichole entered the hospital, she had coffee in the cafeteria. We also know that she didn't see Kari that morning. What we don't know is where she went after she left the cafeteria." Carson took another swallow of his coffee. "Can I get you something to drink?"

Blake shook his head no.

"When Nichole and I talked on Monday night, she made it clear that she knew Keith and Jason had killed Hunter Douglas."

"What the fuck are you saying?" Blake shouted. "My kid would never do that."

"Take it easy, Blake, and let me finish."

Blake leaned back in his chair, crossed his arms over his chest, and glared at Carson.

"Nichole was afraid of them. She had overheard them talking about stabbing Hunter. I should never have allowed her to go back to her house, but she thought she'd be okay. Anyway, after I found her car in the parking lot and no one knew where she was, I decided to dig a little deeper. Taking into consideration the discrepancy between you and Keith, as to what time he arrived at your house, I decided to call the coroner. He told me that determining the time of death isn't an exact science. And, he also said that there was a possibility that Hunter could have been killed earlier than he originally determined."

Blake shook his head back and forth. "No way," he mumbled.

"They did it, Blake. They murdered that kid and Keith tried to frame you for it. I canvased your neighborhood again, asking if anyone saw or heard anything that night. And, guess what? We found someone who remembered something about that night. One of your neighbors mentioned that she saw a kid messing around with your car that night. She heard a car door slam shut and when she looked out her window, she saw a kid walking away. When I showed her a picture of Keith, she said that was the kid she saw. She was about to call you, but, then, he walked away from your car, so she figured no harm was done and ignored it."

"That doesn't prove anything," Blake said defensively. "This is all bullshit. Do you know how crazy that sounds?"

"Totally. Which is why what I'm about to tell you sounds even crazier. Forensics was able to determine that the knife and blood have been in your car since last May. Keith planted it over six months ago and led us to it by telling me that you had moved your car."

Blake stared at him. "I can't believe . . ."

"It is hard to believe, but that's what happened."

"Am I getting out of here?"

"You are. And, I'm sorry for what you've gone through the past few days."

"Nichole heard them talking about killing him?"

"Yes, and I'm really concerned about her. No one has seen or heard from her in days. We've arrested Jason and your son for Hunter's murder. Keith still denies everything, but Jason gave it all up after a few hours of questioning. But, only regarding Hunter Douglas. Both of them deny having had anything to do with Nichole's disappearance."

"And, you don't have any idea where she might be?"

"None. However, I think if we find her car, we'll find Nichole."

"You think she's dead?"

"I'm almost sure of it. They knew she talked to me and I figure they thought if they silenced her for good, they would be in the clear."

"And, you think that Keith did something to Nichole?"

"I think he did, along with Jason's help."

"That's the dumbest thing you've ever said, Carson. There is no way in hell Keith would ever hurt his mother or allow someone else to hurt her."

"I hope you're right. However, she was terrified of both of them. Keith threatened her and told her not to talk to me but she did anyway, and now she's missing. What does that tell you?"

"If any of what you have just told me is true – well, I'd like to see some proof. Nichole could be anywhere. You don't know what happened."

"I know they killed Hunter and I know Nichole heard them talking about it. Put two and two together, Blake. It only adds up to something bad happening to Nichole."

"Would it be possible for me to talk to Keith? Maybe, I can get him to tell me if he knows anything."

Carson sat back in his chair, thinking. "I don't think that will accomplish anything. He tried to frame you for Hunter's murder, so I can't see that he would tell you anything except lies."

Blake shook his head in agreement. "You're probably right, but I figure it wouldn't hurt to try it."

"Let me think about it."

"What I don't understand is why there is no video of Nichole leaving the hospital. Is it possible that she's still there, hiding somewhere?"

Thirty-nine

"We'll be right there," Deputy Truhouse said. "Thanks for calling."

"What's up?" Katts asked.

"That was Joel Nettle, a farmer that lives just off County Hwy P," Truhouse informed the sheriff. "He just found a car on his property."

"Does he know who it belongs to?"

"Nope. That's why he called. He wants to know what to do about it?"

"Did he say how long he figures it's been there?"

"Nope. He just said he was taking a walk in the woods behind his house and saw it sitting there."

"Description?"

"It sounds like it could be Nichole Armstrong's car, Sheriff. He said he peeked inside but didn't see anything," Truhouse told him.

"You mean like a body?" Katts asked.

"Right."

"Well," Katts said, sighing, "Nichole's been missing for almost a week now. If it is her car, let's hope she isn't in the trunk."

Sheriff Katts turned onto County Hwy P and reduced his speed. "He said it was the third road to the left, didn't he?"

"Yeah. It's the next turn," Truhouse said.

Katts turned onto Nettle's driveway, drove about a quarter of a mile, and pulled up in front of an old farmhouse. A man around fifty years of age, wearing an overcoat and an old straw hat walked towards them.

"Mr. Nettle?" the sheriff called out, as he exited his car.

"Sheriff," the man acknowledged.

As they shook hands, the sheriff asked, "When did you find the car?"

"A couple of hours ago. I was out back looking for rabbits and there it was – just sitting there. Damndest thing. I can't figure out how they got it in there without me hearing anything."

"Can you take us to it?" Katts asked.

Nettle looked down at the sheriff's shoes. "You got boots with you?"

"I do."

"Then, I suggest you put them on. There are some pretty deep drifts and you don't want to get those nice shoes all wet."

"Give me a minute," Katts said and walked over to the squad car. "Open the trunk," he yelled to Truhouse. "We need our boots."

Twenty minutes later Nettle, Truhouse, and Katts were staring at a burned car. Katts walked to the rear of the vehicle and looked at the license plate. "It's Nichole's car, all right," he stated. "Let's take a look inside."

Truhouse tried the passenger side door to see if it would open. "It's unlocked," he informed the sheriff."

"How bad is the inside burned?" Katts asked.

"Just a little. It looks a lot worse on the outside." Truhouse replied.

"Clean enough to get fingerprints?"

"I'd say so," Truhouse answered.

"See if you can open the trunk," Katts said.

"Hold on." Truhouse walked to the other side of the car and opened the door. He reached down and pulled the release handle for the trunk.

"It opened," Katts yelled to Truhouse, as he walked to the back of the vehicle. He pushed the trunk up higher and looked inside.

"Is she in there?"

"It's empty," Katts told him.

"Then, where the hell is she?" Truhouse asked. "A person just can't disappear into thin air."

"Get the crime scene unit out here, Mikey. I want them to go over this car with a fine-tooth comb. Someone drove this car here, and I want to know who. Got it?"

"Got it," Truhouse replied, as he pulled his phone out of his pocket."

"Wait a minute," Katts told him.

"What?"

"It might be a good idea to bring in a cadaver dog. See what you can do about that."

"You think she might be out here in the woods?"

"You never know. I think we need to do a check of this entire area. She could be out here," Katts surmised.

"I sure hope not. Let's say a little prayer that Nichole is somewhere safe and sound." Katts murmured.

"Amen, to that," Joel Nettle added.

"Thanks," Truhouse said, as he hung up the phone.

“Did they find any prints?” Katts asked Truhouse. “It’s been almost seven hours since we found that damn car.”

“They found a lot of them. Forensics is running them through AFIS right now. They said they’d call if they get any hits.”

“Mikey, were you the only one who viewed the tapes from Wednesday and Thursday, or did you have help?”

“One of the security guards at the hospital helped. Why?”

“I’d like you to take another look at them. Maybe, something was missed,” Katts replied.

“Where are they? Here or at the hospital?”

“At the hospital.”

“You want me to go to the hospital and look at the tapes from last Wednesday and Thursday?” Truhouse asked.

“That’s right.”

“Now? It’s almost eight o’clock, you know.”

“I guess it can wait until morning. Head over there first thing tomorrow and start looking.”

Truhouse stood up. “Will do. Now, I’m going home. I’ll call you if I find anything on the tapes. It’s gonna take a while, you know?”

“I know. Concentrate on the parking lot, the exits, and the cafeteria. She had to have left that building somehow.”

Forty

"Where's Truhouse? I haven't seen him this morning."

"He went straight to the hospital this morning," Sheriff Katts told Officer O'Reilly. "Hopefully, he'll find something on those tapes."

"Excuse me, Sheriff," O'Reilly said reaching over and picking up the phone. "Officer O'Reilly," he answered. "It's for you." he said, handing Katts the phone, "It's the lab."

"Sheriff Katts, here. Do you have something for me?" He listened for a moment, then, smiled. "You're sure about that?" Katts asked the caller. "That's great news. Can you fax over a copy of that? Thanks." He hung up the phone and looked at O'Reilly, grinning.

"Good news, Sheriff?" O'Reilly asked.

"Yep. I want you to find out where Dr. Campbell is and go pick him up."

"Will do, Sheriff. What's going on?"

"His prints were among those found in Nichole Armstrong's car. I want to know what the hell his prints are doing in her car and why."

"Should I tell him why I'm bringing him in, Sheriff?"

"No. Just tell him I want to ask him a few questions. That's all he needs to know."

"On it, Sheriff," O'Reilly said, as he turned and started to leave the room.

"O'Reilly," Katts yelled.

O'Reilly turned and looked at the sheriff. "Yes?"

"Where are you going?"

O'Reilly looked confused. "I thought you told me to go get Dr. Campbell and bring him in."

"That's right. And, do you know where he is right now?

"Well, I figured he is at the . . . Actually, no," he replied, looking sheepish.

"Well?"

"I'll make some calls, Sheriff."

"Good thinking."

"You want me to get that?" O'Reilly asked when the phone on Katts' desk rang.

"I got it." Katts picked up the phone. "Sheriff Katts."

"It's me, Sheriff."

"Good morning, Mikey. How's it going with the tapes? Have you found anything?"

"The tapes are missing, Sheriff."

"What the fuck are you talking about?"

"The tapes are gone. Either someone took them or they were misplaced. Whatever happened, no one can find them. And . . ." He hesitated. "There's more that I need . . ."

"Spit it out, Mikey," Katts said, after a few moments of silence.

"You need to get over here, Sheriff."

"Why? What's going on that you can't handle?"

"A dead body was found this morning down in the morgue, in one of the cold storage lockers."

"So, what's unusual about that? That's where they keep them, isn't it?"

"Well, Sheriff . . . Well, it isn't one of theirs, Sheriff."

Katts felt his stomach turn as he realized what Truhouse was telling him. "No," he exclaimed.

"Sorry, Sheriff."

Katts fell back in his chair, trying to comprehend the news.

"Sheriff, are you there?" Truhouse yelled. "Sheriff," he yelled into the phone.

"Yeah, I'm here, Mikey," Katts mumbled, after a few seconds. "I'll be right there."

"I have patients to see," Dr. Campbell said, "and, you've kept me here long enough. Unless you intend to charge me with something, I'm leaving."

Sheriff Katts sat back in his chair and stared at the doctor. "No, I'm not charging you with anything and you're free to leave. I have to say, though, Doctor, your explanation is pretty weak."

"Well, weak or not, it's the truth. I drove her car once and it was a long time ago. If my prints were still in her car, then she certainly didn't clean the inside of that car very often. Besides, why would I want to hurt her?"

"Well, I understand you two were pretty close at one time. I also understand that you two got into it and she rearranged your nose. Word is, you really hated her."

Campbell looked at him, shaking his head in disgust. "This is ridiculous. I haven't had anything to do with that woman since she broke my nose. And, before that, we were just friends. So what if I drove her home from the hospital one day? She was depressed over her daughter and I didn't think it was safe for her to drive. And, as I said, it was a long time ago." He stared at Katts. "Are we done here?"

"For now."

“Good!” Dr. Campbell stood up and walked towards the door.

“Wait. There’s one more thing I want to say to you before you leave, Doctor,” Katts said.

Dr. Campbell rolled his eyes and sighed. “What is it now?”

“You can roll your eyes all you want, Doctor. However, no matter what you may think of that woman, as you put it, Nichole Armstrong was a good woman and a good mother. She went through hell after Kari was in that accident and she managed to survive. My God, man, she went through more crap in twenty months than most people endure in a lifetime. And, for what? So that she can be murdered by some sniveling coward? What happened to her is ludicrous and, know this, Dr. Campbell, I will never stop looking for the person who did this to her. You got it?”

Campbell glared at Katts. “Now are you done?”

Katts shook his head in disgust. “Go.”

“By the way, Sheriff, if you have any other questions, call my lawyer.”

“Damn!”

Truhouse looked up from his desk. “Are you okay? You seem pretty angry,” he declared.

“Do I, Mikey? Well, maybe that’s because I am. That damn doctor is an asshole. Acting so high and mighty, like he’s better than everyone else.”

“Hey, he’s a doctor. They all have a God complex. Don’t let him get to you.”

“I know he killed Nichole,” Katts exclaimed. “And, except for a gut feeling and a couple of fingerprints, I don't have one shred of evidence. That bastard is going to get away with it."

"Knowing you, I doubt it."

Katts looked at him. "What do you mean by that?"

"You don't give up. It may take you a while, but you'll eventually find Nichole's killer. And, if it was the doctor, like you think it was, well then . . ." Truhouse hesitated.

"What?" Katts prompted.

"Are you really so sure that Keith and Jason didn't kill her?"

"I don't see them doing it. There was nothing on the tapes that showed they were anywhere near the hospital when she was killed," Katts replied.

"How can we even know that? We don't know exactly when she was killed or how long her body was in that locker before she was found. I think they could have killed her. And, remember, Sheriff, she was stabbed to death, just like that Douglas kid."

Katts shrugged. "That's true."

"Of course, we have no proof," Truhouse reminded him.

"Screw it, Mikey. Right now, for all I know, the hospital chaplain did it."

Forty-one

Nine Months After Nichole's Murder

"I know it's not as large as our old house, but I think you'll be comfortable there," Blake said.

"I'm not going home with you," Kari told him.

"Of course, you are," Blake declared.

"No, I'm not. You aren't my boss. I'm almost twenty years old and I can decide where I want to live. And, it's sure as hell isn't going to be with you."

Blake looked shocked. "But, that's crazy. I'm your father and you need to be with me."

"Do you seriously think I would live with you? Exactly how many times did you visit me while I was in a coma? Ten? Twelve? In over a year and a half, you visited me less than a dozen times. Even now, since I've been out of that stinking coma, you've rarely come to see me."

"What difference does that make now? You're ready to leave the hospital and you need a place to live. Of course, you're coming home with me."

"No, I'm not. I've worked my ass off for the last nine months so I can get out of here and get on with my life. I'm going home – to my house. Grandpa is going to keep making the mortgage payments so I can stay there. If I need any help, like a cleaning lady, they'll take care of it. The fact of the matter is, Dad, they've pretty much taken care of everything for me."

"You can't stay there all by yourself, Kari."

"But, I can and I'm going to. I'm going to get my high school diploma and go to college. Or, maybe I'll just find some nice doctor or lawyer and get married. But, whatever I do, you won't be a part of it."

"But, that's ridiculous."

"There's a theory that people who are in comas can hear people talking. Well, guess what, Dad? It's true. I remember hearing so much when I was in that coma. I remember mom reading to me and my nurse, Betty, singing softly while she bathed me. I know that mom decorated my room for Christmas and that she never stopped talking to me. She was always here with me and now she's gone and I'll never see her again. And, Dad, on rare occasions when you did show up, I heard you . . ."

"What? You heard me what?"

"I heard you say that you wanted me taken off life support. It's too bad that mom was the one to die and not you."

"That's a cruel thing to say, Kari. Besides, I didn't think . . ."

"That I could hear you?" she interrupted. "Well, I could. Do you really think I can live with someone who wanted me to die because I was costing him too much money being alive?"

"No, that's not true. You've got it all wrong, Kari."

Kari laughed. "Do I? God, you're pathetic. Just leave me alone." She rolled over on the bed, turning her back to her father.

Blake waited, hoping she'd change her mind. Finally, he stood up, leaned over, put his hand on her shoulder, and squeezed it. "I'm leaving if that's what you really want. Please, baby girl, remember that I will always be here for you if you need me. I love you."

As her father turned and walked out of the room, Kari wiped away a tear that was rolling down her cheek. Just one more day, she thought, as she closed her eyes and fell asleep.

She turned and glanced towards the door, making sure she was alone in the room. Hesitating for only a moment, she picked up her phone and made a call.

"Dr. Campbell."

"Hi, Ben. It's Kari."

"Hello, Kari."

"I miss you."

"You saw me yesterday."

"I know, but I still miss you."

"You've seen me every day for the past nine months, Kari."

"I'm going home today. I'm finally getting out of this place."

"I know. I'm happy for you."

"My grandparents should be gone by six. Are you coming over?"

"Do you really need to ask? You should know by now that nothing can keep me away from you."

"I'm nervous."

Ben laughed. "Why? What could you have to be nervous about?"

"I don't know. I guess it's because . . ."

"Because what?"

"You know."

"What do I know, Kari?

"Well, it will be the first time that we'll be really alone together. You know what I mean."

“Ah, my sweet innocent little Kari. You need to relax. You have absolutely nothing to worry about.”

“I guess not,” she agreed. “I’m just being foolish. I guess I worry too much, just like mom used to do.”

“Well, Kari, she had a lot to worry about. The poor woman went through hell. But, believe me, you’re nothing like your mother.”

“I’m not?”

“No, absolutely not, except for your looks, of course. Your mother was a beautiful woman and so are you.”

“You think I’m beautiful, Ben?”

“I do. And, Kari, you have nothing to worry about. I’ll take care of everything.”

“You will?”

“Of course. All you need to do is be a good girl, do what I tell you, and everything will be just fine.”

About the Author

I was born in Idaho in 1939. My father's job demanded that we frequently move and, by the age of ten, I had lived in Idaho, Montana, Colorado, Michigan, and Wisconsin.

I am the proud mother of three wonderful sons and two fantastic grandsons. I have no plans to acquire another husband, as they are just too much work.

For most of my life, I worked as an accountant. Two years before I retired, I did a complete switch in careers and managed two Curves fitness facilities in Illinois. I retired in 2002 and moved to Branson, MO. In 2012, I moved to Indiana to be closer to my family and have resided in Highland since then.

I enjoy a good laugh and figure it's my sense of humor that keeps me going when times are tough. Reading has always been one of my passions and I still read a couple of books a week.

In 2014, I wrote my first book, *Blueberries and Bears and My Brother's Shoes*, a book about growing up in the forties and fifties. After I self-published it and gave it to friends and family to read, they encouraged me to get serious about my writing.

I never thought that, at the age of 76, I would become an author. I set a goal for myself to write at least ten books before I die. I've made the ten-plus and I'm pretty sure I have a lot more novels kicking around in this head of mine.

I certainly am enjoying my retirement knowing, when I get up each morning, I have something to look forward to. You can find out more about me and my books at www.susanlpare.com. Please visit me there, sign up to be on my readers' list, and feel free to send me your comments.

For ongoing updates and information regarding Susan and her novels, please visit www.susanlpare.com.

www.ingramcontent.com/pod-product-compliance
Lightning Source LLC
Chambersburg PA
CBHW071856220626
47052CB00002B/144

* 9 7 8 1 7 3 3 5 5 7 2 2 1 *